LINGERING THINGS

DANA NORAAS

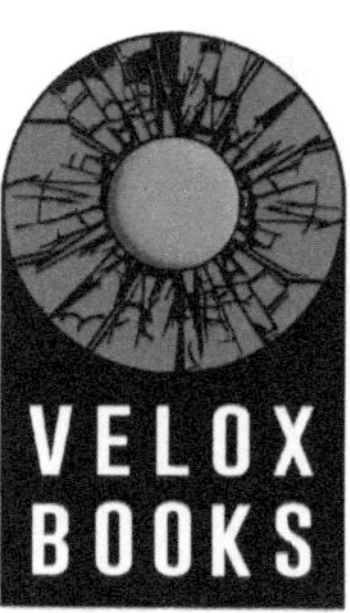

Published by arrangement with the author.

Copyright © 2025 by Dana Noraas.

All rights reserved.

YOU'RE READING ANOTHER TERRIFYING COLLECTION FROM

**FOLLOW VELOX TO KEEP
THE NIGHTMARES COMING:**

For my grandmother, who shared her stories. For my parents, who shared their courage, and for every friend, family member, and stranger who shared their fears with me.

CONTENTS

A WARNING TO THE READER

I HAVE ALWAYS BEEN drawn to all things dark and macabre. To me, *horror* is an umbrella—a genre with many shapes and many faces. All horror fans have their specific tastes and their haunting shadows that lurk behind them. Some readers crave grotesque monsters, rotting zombies, and predatory aliens. Others find their chills in psychotic madmen, sophisticated cannibals, or charming serial killers. Horror doesn't always scream—it unsettles, it lingers, and it haunts in ways that are as personal as fear itself.

Over the years, I've asked countless people, *"What scares you the most?"* A question that always leads to new frights to explore. Because not all horror is the same, and not all terror wears the same face.

When I was in the sixth grade, I purchased the trilogy, *Scary Stories to Tell in the Dark,* written by the late Alvin Schwartz and illustrated by Stephen Gammell. It was my first anthology—a collection of tales that felt like a haunted house to me, every room holding something different. I had to place the book face down on my nightstand after reading certain stories so that the ghoul on the front cover wouldn't watch me sleep. Yet not every story inside wanted to terrify me. Some wanted to play with me, to dance with the idea of horror from a safe, almost whimsical distance.

I wrote this anthology in the spirit of that series. Not to mimic it, but to echo what made it unforgettable—its variety, its surprises, and the unspoken promise that horror can take on many forms.

But I must tell you, dear reader: This book is *not* meant for children. The stories within these pages are not safe and they are not told from a distance.

Know this before you continue: These stories contain graphic violence, including violence of a sexual nature. They explore cruelty, loss, and lasting trauma—the horrors that live inside the human heart, not beneath the bed. I tell you this not to tempt you, but to prepare you. Stories can harm. They can haunt. And they can open doors to places you may not wish to revisit. If you carry scars, some of these pages may press against them. If you carry shadows, some of these stories may feel too familiar as well.

But if you choose to read more, do so with care and know that once these stories find you... *they linger*.

LINGERING THINGS

THE FIRST THING SHE noticed about the house was the smell. It wasn't a bad smell, per se—it reminded her of her old hometown library. *A house,* Jessica thought. The idea made her nervous. More space meant more maintenance. Since she lived by herself, the responsibility of all the yardwork and upkeep seemed daunting. She breathed deeply, and the woodsy scent calmed her. Until now, she had only rented small apartments, but when she saw this house in the ad, she couldn't resist a look.

Jessica had spent her childhood in a quiet, rural area. She couldn't wait to get out of her hometown and move to a city—*any city*—to add excitement to her life. She settled on Philadelphia, where she was accepted at Drexel University for a degree in philosophy. Only about two years after relocating to Center City, the novelty of the hustle and bustle began to wear off. A few months before graduation, she interviewed with a psychological evaluation company based in Boston. They had a local branch in South Philly, where she conducted her interviews and eventually was offered the job.

It didn't pay much, but it allowed her to work remotely while she looked for a more promising source of income. Shortly after accepting the offer, she began to look for new apartments in the suburbs around the city, but her searches yielded few options within her price range. As her search radius grew, the prices fell, and Jessica began to realize how much she missed living in the country.

She found the house listed in a Craigslist ad, and it was located two hours away from the city by car. The ad was not unusual, but for the last line. It read:

HOUSE FOR RENT—$300/mo.
4 BR 2.5 BATHROOMS
3.5 WOODED ACRES
12 MO. LEASE MINIMUM
UTILITIES NOT INCLUDED
PETS ALLOWED, NOT SAFE FOR CHILDREN

At twenty-three, Jessica had no children—only a cat that she had rescued during her first year of college. She named him "Walnut" after the place she found him, the Walnut-Locust subway station. He was seeking shelter from the freezing November rain in the stairwell of the concourse. Scrawny, covered in fleas and city filth, he had a wound on his hind leg that left him with a permanent limp. She had worried that he wouldn't survive the first few days in her care, but he pulled through, and became a fat, loveable tabby. "Locust" would have been a far less loveable name, in her opinion.

The phrase "Not safe for children" seemed peculiar to her. She wondered what made the home unsafe for children. *A sex offender in the neighborhood?* She thought. Possible, but the thought only lingered briefly. The price stood out most to her. There was only one picture of the house in the posting, and it was taken from a distance. She could see that there were some mature pines surrounding the house, but otherwise, Jessica couldn't make out any details. She emailed the rental agent to see if there had been a mistake in the posting and inquired about a visit to the property. The response was almost immediate.

Hello, and thank you for your interest in this property! I can assure you that there has been no mistake in the listed price. This is truly the opportunity of a lifetime! I am conducting an open house next Saturday from 12 PM to 4 PM, and another in July if necessary. My apologies, but we do not make individual appointments to show the house privately. Please let me know if you are interested in attending the June open house!

Sincerely,
Deborah Hayes, Leasing Agent

Jessica decided to make the trip that weekend. As she drove farther from the city, her stress began to melt away into the mountains and trees.

When Jessica pulled into the gravel driveway, a woman wearing a snug, fire-engine-red skirt-suit and heels hustled onto the front porch and greeted her with an oversized realtor smile. She waved her hand wildly, as if there was a chance that Jessica had missed her. Jess groaned inwardly. She distrusted this type of salesperson. Perfectly crisp and flashily dressed, they never have a hair out of place, and always wear expensive and overpowering perfume. They glitter with diamonds, gold, and the occasional Rolex. They epitomize the phrase "dress for success." She supposed that some needed to construct this kind of image to believe that they were capable enough to do their job. Nonetheless, this impeccably-coiffed exterior made the salespeople seem more like selling machines than actual people.

"Hello, you must be Jessica! How great to meet you." The realtor spoke so quickly that Jessica was barely able to mumble a "hello" before the woman continued. "I'm Deborah Hayes." She emphasized her last name with a flourish of her chubby hand and spoke with a jaunty Philly accent. "I am the leasing agent for this property. The couple who was supposed to join us here today just called and cancelled on us. What a pity!" She laughed as if she had told a joke. She paused for a moment, smiling at Jessica, who couldn't help but notice a smudge of lipstick on the woman's front tooth. Jessica felt relieved when she noticed this small fissure in Deborah's façade. It made her more real... *human.*

"Well," Deborah said, "I can tell that you're the quiet type, so let's get to it!"

They began to walk toward the house. "This house was built in 1893. The original owners decided—oh!" The realtor's phone began to ring, and the tone muffled through her purse. "Excuse me, please feel free to look around inside. I'll join you shortly!" She pulled out her phone and began to chirp at the caller, but Jessica barely noticed. She was grateful that Deborah's attention was momentarily diverted.

For only three hundred dollars a month, she assumed that the place would be falling apart, or in need of serious repair, but from what she could see, it appeared sound. She surveyed the surrounding woods, and inhaled the rich smell of pine needles, dirt, and decaying forest matter. She could feel a noticeable drop in temperature as she stepped through the front door. This unnerved her slightly, but she considered that the house probably never got much direct sunlight in this wooded location. She wandered past stairs that led to the second floor and found herself in the kitchen. She was surprised to note that the appliances looked brand new, but the thing that seemed most out of place was a small door in the corner.

The rest of the kitchen had clearly been updated over the years, but it seemed that the owner had never bothered to update the small door that Jessica assumed led to the cellar. It remained in what looked like its original form—almost defiant against the environment of pristine whites and stainless steel. Judging by the few flecks of color around the hinges and the doorknob, the wood had been painted dark green at one point. The thick boards were warped from decades of humid summers and bitter-cold winters, held together by two wrought iron bindings that reminded Jessica of braces on crooked teeth.

"There you are!" Deborah materialized in the kitchen doorway, startling her. "Sorry about that—that was just the owner checking in!" She glanced at the door before returning her gaze to Jessica.

"What's up with that door? It seems..." Jessica began.

"Oh, that old thing leads to the cellar. It should be locked up tight. The owner uses it as storage space for old junk that he refuses to throw away." Deborah walked to the door and tentatively jiggled the handle. "Locked securely, and it will remain that way for the duration of the tenant's lease." Deborah smiled thinly, and Jessica's eyes were once again drawn to the smudge of red lipstick on her tooth.

The realtor turned to lead her back to the hallway and up the stairs. Jessica lingered, looking at the door. There was a small gap between the bottom of the door and the wooden floorboards. Cool air seeped from it the way a person sighs gently in his sleep. Impulsively, she reached out and stroked the door with her fingertips. The sensation gave her goosebumps, despite that it was quite warm that day. *Locked securely.* She eyed the handle, and noticed a single old-fashioned keyhole below the doorknob. She gave it a twist to see for herself that it was locked.

The rest of the house was spacious and had minor wear and tear. They were in the master bedroom upstairs when they heard the crunch of a car in the gravel driveway. "Oh, how perfect!" The realtor exclaimed. "Let me go greet them, and I'll be right back to finish our walk-through. Until then, feel free to continue to explore the rest of the house without me. I'll find you wherever you are." She ended with what Jessica assumed was a "wicked witch" imitation. The realtor squinted her eyes and pointed a hooked finger at her, giggling again before disappearing down the stairs.

Jessica moved to the window to get a look at the new arrivals, who were just stepping out of their green Subaru. "Hello there!

How are you?" She could hear Deborah calling out to them. Her voice was muffled from below, but Jessica could still make out the same overly-cheerful, singsong tone. A man and woman were approaching the front porch, taking in the surroundings, when two young boys burst from the back seat. They charged around their parents, laughing and chasing each other. They disappeared from view, but Jessica could still hear them stomping around on the porch.

"Absolutely not!" She heard Deborah boom. "There are no children allowed!" The sounds of stomping on the porch ceased immediately. Jessica could see the two boys now retreating to their parents, who now stood several feet away from the front steps. Both had the same shocked expression at Deborah's sudden dramatic outburst. "I'm sorry," the father began, "they've had a very long car ride; they're just burning off some energy."

"They're usually very well-behaved," the mother added. Jessica guessed that Deborah must have recomposed herself a bit, because she now spoke in hushed, calmer tones.

"Why can't we just look at the house?" The father was growing agitated. "We drove all the way out here." Deborah must have held firm. A few moments later, the family piled into the car and backed out of the driveway, spraying gravel as they went.

Deborah walked up the driveway and into Jessica's line of sight from where she watched from the bedroom window. She stared after the fading taillights of the family's Subaru until they disappeared from sight. She adjusted her blazer, then turned and stared directly at Jessica.

Jessica quickly backed away from the window. Her heart pounded, and she felt like a reverse peeping tom. She moved into the adjacent bedroom and pretended to be interested in the closet when Deborah rejoined her. She did not mention the other family, but Deborah's outburst was all Jessica could think about for the remainder of the tour.

At the end of the tour, Jessica asked Deborah why the house was listed at such a low price. "The owner only asks that you maintain the house as it is. It's as simple as that. You know how vacant houses always seem to deteriorate faster than those that are lived in. The house has been in his family for generations now, so he can't possibly part with it. Ever since he moved to upstate New York, though, it's easier for him to rent it out at a low price than to let it rot unoccupied." Deborah recited what seemed like a practiced response—one she had used many times before.

"What about it being unsafe for children?" Jessica inquired. Deborah's head turned sharply at this. "You said that you had no children." Jessica shrugged. "I don't, but I was just curious about why the ad specified that. I didn't see anything that looked too dangerous during the tour. And that family that showed up with the boys..."

"It's very unsafe for small children to live out here like this, because they might wander off and get lost in the woods," Deborah said coldly. "The owner was adamant that I include that detail in the posting. That family thought that they could be an exception, but there are no exceptions to Mr. Carroll's rule." She cleared her throat and continued, now in her chirpy voice. "Do you have any other questions?" Her sudden change in tone caught Jessica off guard. "Mr. Carroll? Is that the owner's name?"

"Yes, although he prefers that all communication with tenants be conducted through me." Aside from Deborah's strange behavior, Jessica couldn't find a reason not to apply to rent the house.

Two months later, the lease was signed, the deposits were paid, and Jessica found herself standing in front of her first house. Her car was packed to the roof with everything that could fit. The larger furniture would be arriving tomorrow with her friend Wes, who had offered to help her move on his weekend off from work. So far, she had managed to unload her car and distribute the boxes to the rooms where they belonged. She was in the bedroom upstairs sorting through clothing when she heard a loud *thump* from downstairs. She assumed that it was Walnut messing around in the empty boxes, but she went downstairs to investigate anyway.

When she reached the first floor, the living room was empty. "Nutty!" she called for her cat, adding a few cat-like "pss-psst" sounds. But there was no sign of Walnut, or anything else that could have made the noise. She turned into the kitchen, where her eyes were immediately drawn to the door in the far corner. It was wide open.

Jessica walked to the door. There was no light switch inside the door or anywhere nearby. All she could see were ancient-looking wooden steps that led down into darkness. "Walnut? Kitty-cat?" she called down the stairs. Her throat was suddenly dry, causing her voice to crack. The only response she got was the cool, damp smell of cement and mildew that seeped from the depths of the cellar in an ethereal breath. She shivered and shut the door. She jiggled the doorknob and found that it was locked once more. "Creepy," she muttered to herself, crossing her arms.

It was getting late, and she hadn't eaten more than a few handfuls of chips while unpacking. Jessica heated a can of soup for dinner, expecting Walnut to come running, when he heard the can opener. He did not appear. Later, after she had finished cleaning up, she called for him on the front porch, in case he had slipped outside while she was carrying boxes to the house from her car. She set some food and water next to the front door in case he showed up. She wasn't too concerned, as her biggest fear for the big tabby in the city was that he would wander into a street and be struck by a car. No chance of that happening out here, she thought. Still, it was unusual that he would disappear for so long, especially when food was involved.

Reluctantly, she turned in for the night, exhausted from the day's activity. It felt as though she had only closed her eyes for a minute or two when she was jolted awake by a noise. It sounded like someone was beating the front door slowly and deliberately.

Thump... thump... thump... thump!

She sat up to look at her phone, and she saw that it was barely past midnight. She had only been asleep for a few hours. She listened for a moment. The thumping stopped. She was about to lie back down when something crashed downstairs, followed by inhuman screeches.

Jessica leapt out of bed and ran down the stairs, worried that something heavy had fallen on Walnut. If so, it sounded like he was in a lot of pain. When she turned the corner at the bottom of the stairs, the screeching intensified. She sprinted into the kitchen and came to a halt in the doorway. The cellar door was open again, this time by only a few inches. The screams were, without a doubt, coming from below.

She hesitated to run down the steps blindly in the darkness, so she looked around frantically for a flashlight. The screeching became more frenzied, and she gave up her search, desperate to find the cat. She reached out for the door and yanked it open. The second that her hand touched the door, the screaming ceased abruptly.

Heart pounding, fearing the worst, she called out into the darkness for Walnut, listening intently for a response. The silence seemed deafening. When she reached the top of the steps, she was hesitant to venture into the abyss. Then she heard it. Faint scratchy-scuffling sounds, followed by a heart-wrenching meow, the kind of sound that cats make when they're in the veterinary waiting room. She couldn't go down without a light. She ran back upstairs to grab her phone, picturing poor Walnut trapped and in pain. When she returned to the door, she began her descent without hesitation, calling out for her cat. There was only a quiet mewling response.

She reached the bottom of the stairs and looked around, holding her phone out like a lantern. "Pss-psst, where are you, kitty?" She heard another quiet meow, but muffled this time. This time, she located the direction of the sounds, and she made her way towards them, carefully stepping around old boxes filled with books, glass jars, and an assortment of junk. Everything was covered in a thick blanket of dust. "Walnut..." she called softly.

She heard a noise at the top of the cellar stairs. Walnut stood in the doorway at the top of the steps, rubbing his whiskers nonchalantly on the doorframe with one paw.

"Me-owww..." echoed from the darkness of the cellar.

Jessica stopped dead in her tracks, the hairs on the back of her neck prickling. That meow didn't sound like Walnut—in fact, it didn't sound like any cat. It sounded like a human voice. She took a step back towards the stairs, away from the corner from where the mewling seemed to emerge. "Meoww," it came again, in a strange genderless voice. Jessica bolted for the stairs and scrambled up the steps, every hair on her body standing on end. Behind her, she could hear the meows continue tauntingly, growing louder and less cat-like with each meow. By the time she reached the top of the steps, the voice was screeching the word "MEOW!" over and over, followed by laughter when she slammed the door closed.

She had no money for a hotel, so she packed up Walnut and drove twenty minutes to the nearest parking lot, where the pair spent the night in her car. There was no way she was ever setting foot in that house again.

She woke up to several missed calls and texts from Wes.

5:01 AM

"Hey Jess, heading out now. Should be there around 7 or so..."

5:05 AM

"Just as a heads up, I'm bringing my daughter with me. Her mom asked to switch weekends with me last night."

Jessica saw that it was approaching eight o'clock a.m. *Wes will have been at the house for almost an hour now.* Panic rose in her throat as she peeled out of the parking lot, driving towards the house. She tried to call his phone, but the call went straight to voicemail. She tried a few more times, but to no avail. Then, she tried the realtor's number.

"Hello?" came Deborah's voice over the phone. "Deborah, this is Jessica," Jessica said. "Oh, Jessica! How are you liking the new place?" Deborah asked. "Why didn't you tell me that the house was haunted?" Jessica had no mind for exchanging pleasantries at this point. "What? Oh, dear. I was hoping that you wouldn't have any issues. Did you open the cellar door?"

"It opened itself!" Jessica shouted into the phone. "I spent the night in my fucking car at the church parking lot down the road. My friend and his daughter were supposed to meet me there this morning. I've tried calling him but he's not picking up!"

"His daughter?" Deborah's voice was tight. "How old is she? Listen to me Jessica, do not go back there. It isn't safe—"

But Jessica wasn't listening anymore. She had just turned up the dirt road that led to the house and saw Wes's daughter, Isabelle, standing right in the middle of the road. When Isabelle saw Jessica's car she began to run towards it, screaming and waving her tiny arms.

"Help me!" She shrieked. Jessica pulled over and jumped out of the car. "Izzie, are you okay? It's me, Jessica. Where is your dad?" The girl fell into her arms, crying. "He tried to help you," she said, as she wiped tears from her eyes. "We heard you calling for help. We heard you calling from downstairs." Chills ran down Jessica's back as she thought of the voice that she had heard in the cellar. Isabelle continued, "We went down to help you, but you weren't there. But something else was. Something bad! I got out but my... it got my *dad!*" She sobbed into Jessica's shoulder. "Don't make me go back there, Jessica. Please don't make me!"

Jessica hugged her tightly. "I have to go find your dad. You stay in the car, and Walnut will protect you." She gestured to Walnut, who was watching the pair from the floor of the car's backseat.

Isabelle climbed into the passenger seat of the car and reached to pet the cat, but Walnut let out a low growl and crawled under the driver's seat. Isabelle withdrew her hand and looked at Jessica. "Don't worry, he's a nice kitty. He's just a bit nervous right now." She glanced at Isabelle's tear-streaked face sympathetically. "I'll be right back, I promise."

Jessica set off at a jog towards the house. She wasn't sure exactly what she was going to do, but she had to look for Wes. She saw his truck parked next to the house, still loaded with her furniture. The front door to the house was wide open. "Wes?" She called from the doorway. Silence. From where she was standing, she could see dark marks on the kitchen floor. She continued cautiously towards the kitchen, looking for something that she could use as a weapon. She found a flashlight in one of the boxes in the hallway and flicked on the light. Bright, dependable LED light shot out from the flashlight in a bluish-white beam, giving her some sense of relief.

As she approached the kitchen, she could tell that the cellar door was open before she even saw it. She could feel the cold air and the stench of decay engulfing the first floor of the house. She inspected the marks on the floor and felt a knot in her stomach form as she realized that they were drops of blood. "Wes?" she called again, without any response. With a sinking feeling in her gut, she followed the trail of blood to the cellar door. Even with the flashlight, the inky blackness below seemed impossible to penetrate.

She walked down the steps slowly, ready to turn and run at the first sign of danger. By the time she got to the bottom of the steps, all she could hear was her own heartbeat, thumping away at the base of her throat. She scanned the cellar and gasped when the light fell on a shapeless heap covered by an old blanket in the corner—the blood trail led straight to it. She knew in her heart that it was Wes, even before she was close enough to lift the blanket. Jessica couldn't leave him in the darkness if he was still alive.

She lifted a corner of the blanket and gasped. His face was blackened with death, and was twisted into a horrific grimace, as if he had died in pain. From the looks of it, he had bitten through his own tongue. His hands looked like claws, grasping at his throat, but he had no marks on his neck. The worst of all were his eyes—one had rolled back into his skull, but the other stared straight forward. His gaze seemed to be locked on her. Jessica retched as she backed away in horror. She bumped into a lamp, causing it to fall to the floor and shatter. This snapped her out of her shock, and she turned and ran up the stairs.

She leapt off the porch from the top of the steps and hit the gravel driveway running. Isabelle appeared at the end of the driveway and walked towards her. She walked calmly, which Jessica found strange, given her hysterical behavior only moments earlier. Her eyes widened as she saw the deep claw marks covering Isabelle's arms. "What happened? Isabelle?" Jessica stopped. Behind Isabelle, she could see Walnut's small form lying motionless on the ground near the car. Isabelle only smiled and continued her approach. "Are you okay?" She began to back away, her stomach sinking with dread. Isabelle grinned and spoke in the very voice that Jessica had heard in the cellar the night before. It had no distinctive male or female qualities. It was soft, light, and ageless, and terrifying. "Meowww."

———

Deborah's phone rang for the third time that morning. The first call was from Jessica. The second was from Mr. Carroll. Deborah ignored it. She saw his name on the screen again and didn't dare to ignore two calls in a row. She took a deep breath and answered. "Hello, Mr. Carroll." A quiet but powerful voice responded, "two adults and a child."

"Yes, I am aware of the situation. I've contacted Father Sullivan already. He said that Wednesday was the earliest he could arrange to come out." She paused before continuing. "He told me that it was becoming more difficult to... manage, these past few times. He said that he would need to clear out a full day to be sure."

"Very well." Carrell's voice was calm. He was not surprised that it had gotten stronger. He did not expect that Father Sullivan would be able to survive many more containments. He would need a successor. "The clean-up team is scheduled to do a thorough sweep on Thursday, following Sullivan's visit," Deborah said. "I'll have another advertisement posted by Friday and can begin showing the house as early as Saturday."

"Good."

"It's really a shame," Deborah continued. "She was so *promising*. I will do a better job next time, Mr. Carroll. I really will."

APEX

Anne shivered and pulled her jacket tighter around her. It had to be below freezing, it's always coldest right before the sun comes up. Her fire grew smaller and she knew it wouldn't last much longer. The broken zipper on the jacket did little to help her. It was late spring, but in this climate, it still got cold enough to be a threat. Her leg ached. The bandages wrapped tightly around her thigh stank of old blood and infection. She shifted awkwardly to one side, trying to keep her weight off it. She was sitting at the base of a tall white spruce, leaning against the narrow trunk. Flashlight in one hand, gun in the other, Anne scanned the surrounding brush constantly for movement, ears pricked for any sound. She knew it was still out there; watching her.

Just two days earlier, she had been on a hiking expedition with her husband, Terry. The trip was his idea, as a way for them to get closer to each other. The plan was to hike from Silver Bluff to a small historic mining town about sixty miles away. They had friends who ran a gift shop there and had been begging them for years to come visit. Anne and Terry calculated the hike would take them maybe three or four days at most.

On the first day, they hiked roughly thirteen miles into the Canadian wilderness. Anne had blisters on her feet before they were out of sight of their car, but she didn't complain. By the time they set up a camp for the night, her feet were a bloody mess.

"Jesus, Annie. Why didn't you say anything?" Terry asked when she took her boots and socks off. Anne couldn't think of a logical reason she didn't ask to stop for a break. She wanted to prove herself to him. He pulled some ointment out of his medical pack and applied it gingerly to her sores. She smiled at him. After setting up their tent, they ate sandwiches for dinner. Terry built a fire and the two snuggled together to watch the night sky.

Occasionally, a twig would snap somewhere in the surrounding forest and Anne would jump and peer into the darkness to see what had caused the sound. Terry laughed at this and put his arms around her, reassuring her it was probably just some harmless critter. She felt safe with him. He was an experienced outdoorsman, after all. Since his early teenage years, he had been going on trips like this with his father and uncles. Anne did her best to enjoy this moment with him. She knew it meant a lot for him to include her in this part of his life.

His life. Bitter tears stung Anne's eyes, but did not fall. She hadn't been able to cry since the first night after the attack.

On the second day of their trip, Anne and Terry packed their supplies and set out. Anne's feet were still very tender, so their pace was considerably slower. They trekked for about nine miles before stopping to eat lunch. The spot they chose was beautiful. Broad rocks lined a shallow river. Anne remembered how the air smelled so crisp, scrubbed clean from all the giant trees. She turned to say something to Terry, but his expression stopped her. He was staring past her. She followed his gaze.

A large brown bear stared back at them from the opposite bank, slightly downstream. It was maybe thirty yards away.

"Terry..." Anne started, but he shushed her quietly.

"Don't move." His words were barely audible above the sounds of the water. "Just wait."

Anne had asked him about bears before this trip, but he assured her he had never encountered any on previous excursions. He always brought a gun with him, though.

Seconds felt like hours as the bear gazed at them, sizing them up. Anne's heart was in her throat. It slowly waved its head back and forth in the air, trying to catch their scent. When at last it looked like it was about to carry on, Anne heard a small grunt from their side of the river. She heard Terry curse as she turned to see what made the noise, but part of her already knew.

Two small cubs ambled along in the shallow water, oblivious to Anne and Terry's presence. She glanced back at the adult bear, the mother. Her body language was entirely different now.

"Anne, we need to go right now," Terry spoke quietly. "Slow." He added urgently, "Just back up with me. Leave everything. Don't turn your back."

Anne's body felt numb. She put the rest of her sandwich down and began to shuffle backwards on the rock, copying Terry's moves. The sound of their movement caught the attention of the cubs, and they started to approach with caution. Tears were rolling down Anne's cheeks as they came closer, sniffing at the discarded food and backpacks. They were so close. *Stay there, cubs.* She prayed silently. The one cub seemed content to investigate their food and supplies, but the larger one was more interested in the two creatures backing away slowly. He bounced closer.

Anne's eyes went back and forth from the cub to its mother. She was also making her way across the river now. Anne panicked. She got to her feet abruptly, scaring the cub. It cried out and retreated to its sibling.

"Anne, no!" Terry yelled. But it was too late. The mother was already at a full charge. Water flew from her fur in every direction. Anne grabbed at Terry's arm and tried to pull him up. She could hear the mother bear grunting as she bounded closer behind her.

Pain exploded through her leg as the bear struck her right thigh with a massive paw. Anne fell to the side. The bear then fell upon Terry, who was still mostly on the ground. She pounded his chest with the weight of her upper body, biting and clawing at his face and arms. Anne heard a sickening crunch as the bear bit into his shoulder.

Terry was screaming and flailing. Punching desperately at the bear's nose and eyes, his legs trying to push her weight off of him. The bear caught one of his punches in her jaws and crunched down hard, causing Terry to shriek. The sound made Anne sick as she watched in horror. She wanted to help him. She wanted to kick at the bear's face and beat it to death with a large stick. She wanted to go grab the gun out of his backpack by the river. But as Terry's screams grew more intense, Anne turned and ran.

At that moment, she did not feel the pain from her boots. She did not feel the pain from the gash on her thigh. Instead, she felt her soul dying. She felt the ground beneath her feet and the air she gasped for. Guilt and terror filled her mind. She left Terry to die. Behind her, she heard him scream one last anguished cry that was cut short. She kept running. With her lungs on fire and her mind screaming a thousand terrible things at her, she finally broke. She took a few final staggering steps before she collapsed to her hands and knees. She threw up the few bites of her sandwich that she had eaten earlier and continued to retch even after her stomach was empty.

Anne almost caught her breath when she heard something moving through the woods. It didn't sound too close, but she couldn't let herself stay there. She made it to her feet and continued at a fast jog. If it was the bear, she didn't want to alert it to where she was by crashing around in her heavy boots. This time, she was very much aware of how much her feet and leg hurt. She hobbled on as fast as she could, favoring her injured leg. She couldn't tell where the trail was anymore. She had just run blindly through the woods earlier.

She stepped on a stick that made an impossibly loud crunch, making her heart race again. If that bear was following, surely, she would've heard that. Anne quickened her pace again, unsure if she was heading back toward civilization or further into the forest. A root caught her foot and sent her sprawling. She tried to catch her balance on a sapling, but it bent easily, and she continued to fall down the steep incline. Rocks jutting from the ground bit into her body as she tumbled down the ravine. Young pine branches slapped at her face and hands as she tried to break her fall. The last thing she saw was a large rock bed rising up from the slope to meet her.

Anne woke to a light rain soaking through her clothes. Her entire body was screaming complaints at her. She sat up, rubbing her head. When she pulled her hand away, she saw blood on her hand. Not wet, but sticky. She saw the rock she had hit her head on when she fell. Her eyes darted over her surroundings, looking for the bear, but her vision was blurry. She could hear the river nearby, which made her nervous. She wasn't far from where they first saw the bear. The sound of the water and the rain, which she once found peaceful, covered any sounds of approaching noises.

She winced when she tried to stand. Her thigh where the bear had clawed her felt hot to the touch. The cuts were deep, still oozing dark blood. Anne took her jacket and shirt off to use the shirt as a bandage. She used her teeth to tear her shirt into strips to wrap around her thigh to stop the blood. Shivering, she pulled her jacket back on over her undershirt. The zipper was broken, probably from the fall.

The sun was getting low, and the temperature was dropping. Anne's body ached. She searched her pockets. All her supplies were in the backpacks she and Terry had left behind. Cell phones, cold-weather gear, the tent, flares, a hatchet, food. *The gun.* The only things she had in her pockets were Chapstick, a pen-sized flashlight, and a Swiss Army knife that she'd had since she was seven years old. The dull knife was maybe two inches long at most. She'd rarely ever used it except to dig dirt out from under her fingernails. She'd never had to use it for anything more.

Slowly, Anne got to her feet. The pain from her raw blisters was back with a vengeance. The bear would've found her by now if it was following her, she told herself. Through the clouds, she estimated that the sun was setting to her right. That gave her rough coordinates, at best. She had no idea where the closest town was, or where she was in relation to it. She decided that her best chance was to find shelter for the night and to set out in the morning to try to find the trail.

She made her way toward the river; her throat was scratchy and dry. At the edge of the woods, she looked around in the growing darkness. She could see the stream ahead, but getting to it would put her out in the open. She needed water badly, so she had to take the chance.

Anne hobbled to the bank of the stream and scooped the icy water into her mouth. She smiled as she realized how something that tastes like nothing could be the most delicious thing in the world at the same time. Once she drank her fill, she retreated to the cover of the forest. She knew she should have washed her injuries but couldn't imagine stripping down without a change of warm dry clothing or clean bandages. She found a downed tree and settled in against the upturned roots. It wasn't great protection, but it was slightly warmer, and it protected her from the rain and wind. She sat for a moment before her terror and emotions overwhelmed her. She curled up and sobbed into her hands as quietly as she could. Everything had gone so horribly wrong so fast.

She fell asleep at some point, but the pain in her thigh kept her from sleeping very long. She drifted in and out during the night, waking up whenever she heard a noise. Once she woke and heard something moving amongst the fallen leaves, crunching on small twigs. It had stopped raining, but it was so dark she couldn't see her own hand in front of her face, so she just froze. She thought about the penlight in her pocket but decided against it. Terrified, she listened as whatever animal was making the noises moved farther away. She stayed awake for the rest of the night.

When morning came, Anne breathed a sigh of relief. Over the past few hours, she had been forming a plan of action to get herself to safety. First, she would follow the stream until she found the backpacks and supplies. She could clean her wounds then with actual medical supplies, eat, and get warmer clothing. She would also find Terry's gun and their phones. She knew it was risky and dangerous to return to that spot, but she had no choice. There's no way she could survive at this point without those supplies. From there, she could follow the trail back to where they parked their car.

Anne paused, thinking about the attack. *I left Terry.* She brushed thoughts of him out of her mind. She had to focus on surviving.

Anne crawled out from her makeshift shelter and stretched. She felt shaky on her feet, which didn't come as a big surprise. Considering the amount of heat her thigh was giving off, she knew it was most likely infected. She was grateful, though, that she had broken no bones. She forced herself to remove the bandages and rinse the gashes with cold water from the stream. The cloth stuck to her skin, making her eyes water when she tried to unwrap it. She had to splash water onto her thigh to get the crusted blood and pus to soften enough to allow her to remove the bandages. The smell was worse than the pain. Fresh blood started to flow once the scabs were removed, so she worked quickly. She did her best to wash the cloth before wrapping her thigh once more.

Another thought dawned on her, as her bladder casually reminded her of its existence. How was she going to pee? Squatting was out of the question, considering the state her thigh was in. Fortunately, there were a few young trees nearby that held her weight, so her arms did most of the work. Of all the things she learned in college, who would've guessed that was the thing to come in handy right now?

Anne set out to find her supplies, walking upstream. She didn't have to travel far before she saw the bright orange of her backpack on the rocks up ahead. Her mood quickly changed from excited to crushed as she got closer and saw it had been torn apart. Terry's bag was nowhere in sight. She searched the torn remnants of her bag and found all her food was gone or destroyed. She found her cell phone, little good it did her. The rain had turned it into a glorified skipping stone. All the rice in Asia couldn't revive it.

Her medical kit was still there, sealed in its waterproof box. Without waiting, she pulled her pants off. She had to take her boots off first, which was almost as painful as unwrapping her thigh bandaging. She did her best to quickly clean the wound on her thigh and bandage it with her meager supplies. Her feet were bloody and raw, but there wasn't much she could do for them besides changing her socks. She put on her warm gear hastily and immediately felt better. Their tent bundle was torn and beat up. From the looks of it, shelter from the elements was beyond its capabilities.

Anne also found two flares that were left untouched, along with a flashlight, a box of waterproof matches, and her thirty-two-ounce water bottle. In nearby shrubs, she noticed shreds of the blue fabric from Terry's bag. Avoiding looking toward his body, she rummaged around in his bag. She couldn't find Terry's phone, but she did find his gun safely wrapped in his clothing. She also recovered his monogrammed silver flask, which still had a decent amount of whiskey left in it.

She had never shot a gun before, but the weight of it in her shaking hand made her feel better. Careful to keep her fingers off the trigger, she inspected it and pushed the button that released the clip. She counted the bullets and saw that there were only seven. Anne knew if Terry's phone wasn't in his bag, he must have had it in his pocket. She checked her surroundings again, the sound of the stream making her paranoid. That's when she noticed Terry's body was gone.

Her empty stomach twisted when she realized why it was gone. Her eyes wandered over the spot she last saw him. Despite the rain, there was still a lot of his blood in a concentrated area, but no other remains. She would have to walk past it to follow the path back to Silver Bluff. She knew she would not make it all the way back in one day, but might run into other hikers as she got closer.

With her water bottle full, she started down the trail. When she got to the spot where Terry had died, she paused and said a quick prayer for him.

"I'm so sorry I left you," she whispered with her head bowed. As she forced herself to look at the blood on the ground, she noticed something odd. The pine needles and mud had some marks that indicated he was dragged off. By the bears, she assumed, but there were also blood droplets in the drag marks. Not smears of blood, perfectly round drops.

Anne slowly raised her head and saw more marks and smears on the tree trunk next to where Terry had fallen. She continued up the tree. If she'd had anything in her stomach besides water, Anne would have thrown up again.

Above her in the branches, was Terry. What was left of him, anyway. The flesh had been stripped off of more than half of his face. Some of it was dangling in strips. One of his eyes was missing or crushed in. It was hard to tell with all the blood. The other eye bulged out and stared blankly at her. Anne couldn't look away. Terry's chest was ripped open, with his exposed ribs hooked onto the branches. His intestines dangled like Spanish moss.

Anne finally looked away, retching, when she realized he no longer had the lower half of his body. Did bears usually store food in trees? Anne was no wilderness expert, but she knew that bears aren't the only meat-eaters in the woods. She scanned the ground once more. She easily identified the tracks made by the bear, from the size and claw marks. Then she noticed slightly smaller tracks and chills ran down her back as she came to the conclusion that they were cat prints. *Large* cat prints.

She had to keep moving. Anne wiped at her nose and started walking down the trail at a brisk pace. At least her thigh was feeling a little better since she dressed it properly. It was a beautiful sunny day; perfect for hiking, but she couldn't enjoy it. She kept expecting the bear to show up, or a mountain lion, or even Bigfoot at this point. She kept her eyes moving constantly to search for any signs of danger.

She took small sips of her water regularly as the day went on, balancing her dehydration with rationing her supply. She had contemplated emptying Terry's flask to fill with more water, but ultimately decided against it. *Drink responsibly,* she thought dryly.

After a few hours of walking in silence, she began to feel better. Less paranoid, now that she had put some distance between herself and where they had been attacked. She watched squirrels bounce through the woods, listened to the birds singing. Then she heard it. The distinct crunch of something large walking through the woods nearby. Anne froze, her heart pounding. The crunch of fallen leaves and pine needles continued off the path to her left. Slowly, she pulled the gun out of her coat pocket. Whatever was making the noises was getting closer. She could see something brown making its way through the bushes. Anne pointed the gun in its direction and placed her finger on the trigger.

A deer poked its head out from behind a group of trees. A small spotted fawn stood by her side. Anne breathed a sigh of relief and dropped her arms to her sides. The deer watched her for a moment, then decided to turn and disappear back in the direction they came from. As Anne's heart rate slowly returned to normal, she put the gun back into her pocket and continued to walk.

She had no idea how many miles she had traveled by the time the sun began to sink. Her legs ached and her stomach growled relentlessly. She cursed herself for not staying longer near the stream to look for more supplies or at least a can of food. She did not trust herself to eat any mushrooms, although she saw quite a few that looked reasonably safe. She took a swig from the flask instead and grimaced at the taste. Not the smartest idea perhaps, but the whiskey warmed her up and gave her a little more energy to carry on.

As it grew darker, she had to decide to either continue walking through the night or find shelter. As much as she wanted to push herself and keep walking, she knew her legs would eventually give out on her and she would be left too exhausted to find shelter in the darkness. She searched the forest on the sides of the trail to see if there was anything she could use. The forest had little to offer her. At best, she could drag a few fallen branches to lean against the base of a bigger tree.

Once she had constructed her rustic lean-to, she gathered up small twigs and pine needles to start a fire. It wasn't completely dark yet, but the sunlight was fading quickly. Her hands shook as she struck a match. Once the flame took, she hurried to grab more branches to feed it. As her fire grew, Anne had to venture further away to gather more wood to burn. She hadn't even thought to look for Terry's hatchet after she found his gun. *Stupid!* She gritted her teeth as she limped through the woods looking for branches small enough to carry or drag back to her fire.

Each time Anne returned with more firewood, the fire was struggling to stay alive, and she had to hurry and throw on most of the wood she had just collected to keep it burning. She was about to go get more wood when she thought she saw something moving amongst the trees. Anne stopped and peered out past the fire into the forest. It was still light enough to just make out shapes, but everything had turned dusky gray.

Anne pulled out her flashlight and shined the beam into the woods. A pair of eyes reflected the light back at her. She gasped and grabbed for the gun. The mountain lion stood at a distance, but still too close for comfort. It blinked slowly and disappeared silently into the darkness. Anne stared after it for a few minutes, unsettled by how quietly it moved through the foliage. Out of the corner of her eye, she could see the fire was hungrily burning through the last of the pile of branches she had thrown on it. She had to get more; she had to keep that fire burning. Anne took another swig of whiskey from the flask.

She could hold either the flashlight or the gun. She needed one arm free to collect firewood. Tucking the gun back into her pocket, she set out in the opposite direction she saw the mountain lion go. She couldn't help but feel like she was a beacon in the darkness, with her flashlight and loud footsteps signaling to all the animals in the forest. Fortunately, she found a few smaller logs that would last longer on the fire. Once she had gathered all she could carry, she turned to head back to the fire.

The mountain lion was back. It stood a few yards away now, between her and her camp. The sight of it made her drop her firewood. Keeping the flashlight aimed at its face, she pulled the gun out. "Get out of here! Get!" she shouted at the big cat, hoping to sound more threatening than she felt. The mountain lion watched her, the tip of its tail flicking back and forth. She had seen this behavior before in domestic cats and did not like seeing it now.

Anne pointed the gun at the cat, flashlight still focused on its face. "I said get out of here!" she cried again. The mountain lion casually looked at the fire over its shoulder, and then back at Anne. It took a step in her direction.

Anne fired a shot at it but missed. Her hands were shaking so badly. The cat didn't hesitate and bounded off into the darkness. A terrible thought came across Anne's mind as she hastily grabbed her firewood and returned to the safety of the fire. *It's stalking me. It's waiting for me to sleep.* She had seen videos on the internet of people being stalked by cougars and the like. They don't mind playing the long game.

She would burn the branches of her lean-to before going back into the surrounding darkness if she had to. Anne took another pull from Terry's flask. The whiskey burned going down but was a welcome, if not fleeting, source of heat. She dozed off once or twice, only to wake with a jolt when she heard a noise.

The first time it was just the fire crackling, which prompted her to pile more wood on. The second time, she was convinced it was something else. She swept the surrounding trees with her flashlight, expecting to see those eyes staring back at her. Nothing. Her firewood supply was getting low. She had already started to burn the branches from her lean-to. If she could keep this fire alive until daybreak, she should be okay.

After a moment of deliberation, Anne threw the remaining branches of her shelter onto the fire. They weren't doing much to protect her at this point anyway. She leaned back against her spruce tree and tried to sleep, confident the flames would keep the mountain lion at bay long enough for her to get some sleep. Before nodding off, she made sure the gun was on her lap one last time.

She woke to a throbbing pain in her thigh. Her fire was dwindling, and the sky was just barely getting lighter. She felt relieved, knowing it would soon be light enough for her to move, until she saw its face. The mountain lion crouched across the dying flames. In the dim lighting, its face looked ghoulish. Pale fur on its face contrasted with its black eyes. Anne fumbled for the gun, but the mountain lion was already moving the second she broke eye contact. She had no time to stand up. She raised the gun as it reached her, but the impact knocked the gun out of her hand.

Claws and teeth tore at her arms as she tried to defend herself. *This is it,* she thought. She screamed as the mountain lion tried to reach her neck. She rolled to her side to keep her stomach and throat away from the mountain lion's reach. Massive paws raked her back, causing her to scream again. She couldn't see where the gun had fallen, but the emergency flares were right there. She grabbed one and popped the cap off. Bright red flames shot out of the end and she stabbed behind her head with it. She must have made contact with the mountain lion because she heard it yowl, but it didn't relent. She rolled once more so she could see it, and the flask fell out of her jacket pocket with a clink.

Now that she was facing the mountain lion again, it hesitated, eyeing her hungrily. Keeping her eyes locked with the mountain lion, Anne reached for the second flare and lit it. The cat took a step back but did not flee. She threw the first flare at it, screaming at it to leave her alone. She could see singed fur from her frantic flare stabs on its head near one of the eyes. It was waiting again. Just as it knew the fire would eventually die, so would her flares.

The light from the flare she threw let her see where the gun had fallen: slightly to the right of the mountain lion. Thinking quickly, and desperately, Anne took the flask and filled her mouth with whiskey. Then she slowly got to her feet, wincing from the old wounds and the new.

Fuck these fucking animals. Fuck these woods. Fuck all of this.

Holding the flare at arm's length between her and the mountain lion, Anne inhaled deeply through her nose and lurched forward, spraying the whiskey at the cat. The mountain lion's face didn't burst into flames like she expected, but it sure didn't like the whiskey in its eyes and nose. She continued forward, stabbing at the distracted mountain lion with her flare, hoping the whiskey would light.

Anne's leg gave out as she took another painful step forward, but she was right where she wanted to be. She grasped the gun as she fell and rolled to her side. She fired two shots as the mountain lion turned to face her. The first shot landed in its shoulder, but the second one hit the center of its chest. It screamed at her and moved to attack again, but it fell to the ground before it could take a step. Anne screamed and fired the remaining four bullets into its head. She kept clicking the trigger well after she was out of rounds.

After she was certain the cat was dead, she rolled onto her back, panting. Even if she wasn't going to be cat food, she knew she probably still wouldn't make it out of the forest alive. Her arms and back were shredded, and she had a large gash down the side of her face. Despite the adrenaline coursing through her body, she felt cold. She felt like she was dead already. She closed her eyes, ready to join Terry.

"Hey there," a man's voice called from somewhere in the forest. Anne's eyes popped open.

"Are you okay?" The voice came again. Anne struggled up onto her elbows and saw a flashlight sweeping around through the trees.

"Help!" Anne croaked. "Help me, I'm over here!" She called again, louder this time. There were more voices now, getting closer. Anne grabbed the flare off the ground and waved it over her head. Her vision blurred, but she could see two figures running through the woods toward her. They seemed to be moving in slow motion, still so far away. Anne put her head back down and closed her eyes, warm relief washing over her. Anne was no longer cold.

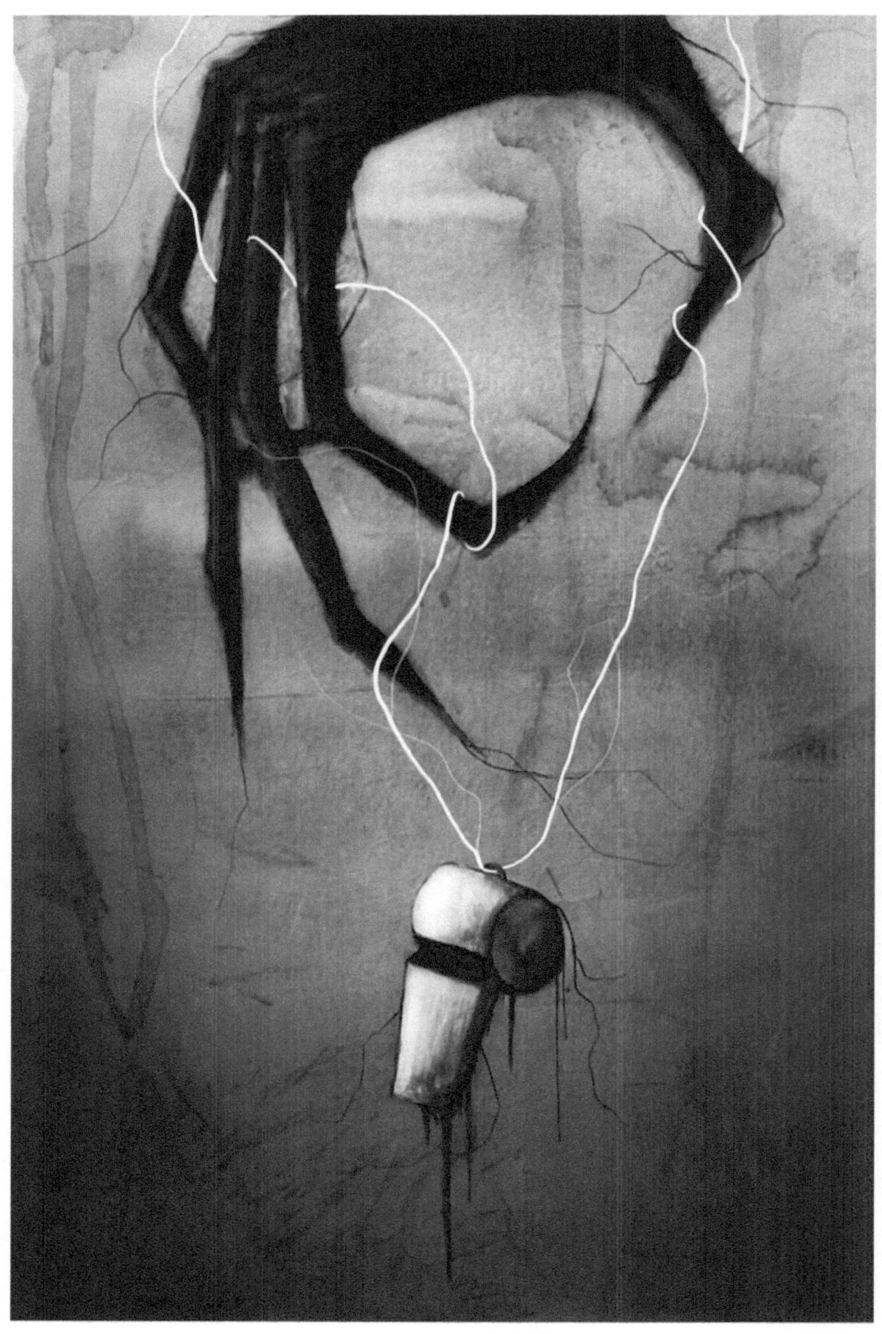

WHISTLE FOR ME

J ANET MYERS BRUSHED SOME stray hair out of her eyes as she struggled to focus on her book. She had recently started a new medication that sometimes made her drowsy. Around her, children ran and squealed with joy in the sunlight. Her son, Robbie, was engaged in some game about pirates. She smiled as she watched him sword fight with another young pirate near the slides. He was a timid and shy boy, so it always made her happy to see him making friends.

Robbie had a few small developmental delays, and she dreaded the day he might be made fun of for them by his peers. A small silver whistle hung around his neck like a badge of courage. One day he had gotten upset and scared when he couldn't find her at the grocery store. He knew not to speak to strangers, so when an employee at the store tried to help, he kicked him in the shin and ran screaming. It was chaos at the hands of a toddler. That night, as Janet tucked Robbie into bed, she placed the whistle around his neck.

"If you're ever scared and you need me, I want you to blow into this whistle and wherever I am I will come to you." She raised it to her lips and gave it a quick *toot toot*, which made him smile.

"Just remember you have to save this for when you *really* need me. You remember the story about the little boy who cried wolf, right, Robbie?" she asked. Robbie nodded solemnly. He seemed to understand her. Since she gave him the whistle, he had only used it once—when he saw a spider in his room. Except for bath time, he never took it off.

Janet rubbed her eyes and looked back to her book. Her medication didn't usually affect her too severely; maybe it was all the sun. She closed her eyes for a moment and decided it was time to head home—a short walk from the park. She stood up as her eyes struggled to readjust to the brightness. Robbie was no longer by the slide. She glanced around the playground, looking for his red shirt, his face. Listening for his laugh. Her pulse quickened as she failed to locate him.

"Robbie, time to go home!" she called, waiting for him to emerge from a tube or playhouse. "Robbie?" she called again with a note of concern in her voice. One of the nearby mothers looked up, then immediately scanned the children for her own child. Janet jogged around the playground, getting concerned looks from other parents as she became more panicked. "Robbie!" she cried when she couldn't find him. "Where are you?" One couple approached her.

"Can we help you?" the husband asked.

"My son, Robbie. He was just playing by the slide and now I can't find him. He's not..." Her sentence was cut off. Above the chatter and noise from the children, a whistle was blasting. Tears sprung without invite to Janet's eyes and she felt a copper taste at the back of her throat.

"That's him! That's—that's his whistle," she said to the couple. Her voice was tight with fear.

"Robbie!" Janet yelled as she ran toward the sound. It was coming from the far side of the tall chain-link fence that surrounded the playground. At the bottom, there was a corner where the fence had been pulled back just enough for a small child to crawl through. The whistle kept screaming, but she couldn't see him anywhere in the dense trees beyond the fence. She tried in vain to pull the fence back further, so she could get through, cutting her hand in the process.

When the other parents saw her running back to the entrance gate, they already had their phones out to call for assistance. The whistle cut off just as Janet reached the other side of the fence.

Janet tore through the overgrown weeds at the edge of the trees with no regard for thorns or poison ivy. She screamed Robbie's name repeatedly as branches snapped at her face and arms. By now, the other park-goers had gathered around on the playground side of the fence. The parents watched in horror as one of their worst fears came to life in front of their eyes, clutching their children to their sides as if they too, might vanish. A few parents joined her in searching the trees for any sign of Robbie.

By the time the police showed up, Janet was covered in blood and dirt, still screaming her son's name. One father who came to help her made the mistake of telling her to calm down. Janet slapped him in the face. She was never one for violence, but losing her son made her wild, like a feral cat.

One of the kids at the park that day was my friend Andy. His mother took him and his younger sister home after speaking to the police. She hadn't seen anything worth mentioning. He told me the story the next day at school, although I had heard several renditions of it by the time lunchtime came around.

We were both in the second grade, a few years older than Robbie, who was in kindergarten. The reality of the situation struck sobriety into my classmates that nobody at Wharton Elementary had ever seen before. Teachers tried their best to distract us with fun activities to prepare for the upcoming summer vacation, but had little success. The disappearance of Robbie Myers was on their minds, too—and we could sense it.

The school held an assembly that Friday. Students from kindergarten through the third grade were marched single file into the auditorium after the morning announcements. The guidance counselor, Miss Abby, conducted a brief seminar on "Stranger Danger." Following after was a slightly improvised demonstration of basic self-defense, taught by the gym teacher and a few brave volunteers from the crowd.

The older kids rolled their eyes and cracked jokes about the assembly and how stupid it was. I wanted to impress them, although I was a whole year younger. I was about to blow the most intense raspberry I've ever managed with my seven-year-old lungs (you know, the kind where you line up the bases of your palms in the center of your mouth and let a long juicy one rip) when a new woman stepped onto the stage in front of us. It was Robbie's mom.

I never really knew Robbie, but listening to his mother talk about him, I felt as though I did. When she told her story about the day he went missing, I imagined how my own mom would react in the same situation. Her voice wavered a few times as she spoke about searching for her boy, causing a lump to form in my throat. I learned a lot about empathy at that moment and was glad I didn't get the chance to blow that raspberry.

Months passed, and no one could find any sign of Robbie. The police said it must have been some kind of animal that dragged him off. Whatever it was, no traces or clues were left behind. My mom told me they used cop dogs to find his scent, but every time the dogs were brought to the place Robbie disappeared, they just barked and bayed and pulled their trainers in circles. Nothing like this had ever happened in our town before.

A service was held in Robbie's memory one weekend as the summer heat faded. I went with my parents and saw that most of the faculty and students from my school also attended. I saw Andy with his family and waved to him. He waved back, but stayed by his mother's side. The parents hovered over their children, barely letting them out of arm's reach.

As school started up, some parents were still reluctant to let their children out of their sight. Many drove their kids and walked them to the front doors. With my new third-grade status, I convinced my mom to let me take the bus and assume my rightful place in one of the back seats with Andy. The more time passed without incident, parents gradually relaxed and everything seemed to be back to normal. More and more of our friends rode the school bus regularly again.

One day in early October, I got off the bus at Andy's stop to play at his house for a few hours. My mother had to work late at the hospital that day and didn't want me to be home alone. Andy's house was always exciting for me. He had two older brothers and a little sister who had just started kindergarten. As an only child, I loved the craziness of being in a house full of people. There was always some sort of fight between the siblings and Andy's mom was frazzled by four o'clock. On the occasions I was there for dinner, we had pizza delivered, and Andy's mom had wine. I'd only met Andy's dad once when he was home briefly between work travels. He was nice to me, but I stayed out of his way regardless.

That night we had tacos instead of pizza, which was fine with me. Afterward, I thanked Andy's mom for dinner and gathered my things to go.

"Is your mom home yet?" she asked, clearing the table.

"Yeah, probably. She's usually home by six," I said casually, not fully knowing. It was half-past seven at this point and getting dark outside.

"Maybe I should drive you home—" she responded, but was interrupted by the sound of a crash followed by crying in the living room. "Marcus!" She yelled toward the commotion, a bowl of salsa still in her hand. "Why is your sister crying?"

I shrugged my backpack onto my shoulders.

"It's okay," I assured her as I made my way to the door. "It's only one street down. Plus, I'm gonna be eight soon anyway. I can go by myself." But she was already in the other room, scolding Andy's older brothers for whatever had happened. I said a quick bye to Andy and went out the door.

The cool air outside excited me as I started my trek home. I *was* old enough to walk by myself, I told myself. I started down the sidewalk with confident steps, but by the time I got to the corner of the block, the street lamps came on. The shadows grew larger and darker, and my mind politely reminded me of all the scary things that may lurk within them. I maintained my pace, more out of fear than confidence now. I had to walk past the playground to get home.

I could see the corner of my street up ahead and focused on that like it was a beacon of safety. As I walked past the park gates, I couldn't help but think of Robbie and his mother speaking at the assembly. I was much older than he was now. I could put up more of a fight if someone tried to kidnap me. Or some*thing*. That last unwelcome thought popped into my head before I could push it away, sending goosebumps down my arms. I stared straight ahead, worried I might see Robbie's ghost playing on the swing set. I finally got to the edge of the park's fence and felt a small wave of relief now that I was past the park. A smirk formed on my face. I wasn't a chicken after all. Then something rustled in the bushes next to me and a bird burst out of the foliage, causing me to jump back and let out a yelp. In an instant, my heart was in my throat. All my stoic resolve was gone. I stared at the bush as if waiting for more birds to fly out and attack me. Then I saw the eyes.

It felt like my body had been flushed with ice water. Through the gaps between the leaves and branches, I saw two eyes staring at me from inside the bush. My mouth went dry. A large bony hand protruded from the shrubs towards me, beckoning me to come closer. A shiny silver whistle dangled from the fingers like rosary beads. I backed away into the street quickly. Too quickly, my foot slipped on the curb, and I went sprawling onto my back. My head hit the asphalt, and I struggled to crawl backward. In cartoons, when a character is hit on the head, they see stars circling around them. Instead of bright stars, my vision was obscured by shadowy circles, making things darker and blurry. I could see the monster slowly emerging from the bushes on all fours. A big, toothy grin spread across its elongated face as it approached. Its pale eyes were fixated on me and never blinked. I closed my eyes and the last thing I heard was a horrific screech.

I woke up on the couch in my living room. I looked around and saw my mother standing over me, with her phone held against her ear.

"He's awake now, he's awake," she said into the phone, her voice trembling. "Could you please? I just want to make sure he's okay." A pause. "Thank you, Sharon. Thank you so much. I'll see you later. Goodbye." She hung up the phone and crouched beside me, brushing my hair off my forehead. "Sweetie, are you okay? What happened? You scared me so bad. Can you sit up?" I sat up and she took a penlight out of her shirt pocket and flashed it across my eyes. She grabbed my head and kissed my forehead. "I'm so sorry I was late. I was on my way to pick you up from Andy's and I saw you laying in the middle of the street. I've never been so scared in my life!"

"Me, too," I mumbled, still dazed. "I fell off the sidewalk. Something... something scared me." I struggled to remember what I saw. "Some birds flew out of the bushes and the..." I trailed off. *Those eyes.* "Mom, there was a monster in the bushes. It scared the birds out and I saw it there. It tried to get me!" My mom cocked her head.

"What kind of monster?" she asked. "A dog?"

I shook my head.

"No, it had hands, like a person. With long fingernails. It had a whistle with it," I said.

My mom's eyes widened. She pulled her phone out and went into the kitchen, leaving me alone on the couch. I could hear her speaking to someone, describing what I had just told her. I heard Robbie's name. Then I heard a faint tapping sound. I looked to the window, where the sound was coming from. It was dark outside now and I couldn't see much. I moved closer, cautiously, as the tapping sound continued. I felt my stomach sink to the floor when I saw what was making the noise. Outside the window, a silver whistle hung from our rose bushes, tapping against the glass.

CONSIGNMENT

Last night was the last straw. I know. I've told myself this lie before, but as I applied concealer to my swollen and tender cheekbone in the mirror, I knew this was it for real. Josh would be at work until 5:00 and stay out for drinks until 8:00 or so. He'll come home to a barren apartment. I'd already purchased my tickets and contacted my college roommate, Morgan. She offered me the spare bedroom at her place in New Orleans. We had a few small differences in the past, but she was giving me an easy out. All I had to do was grab my bags and leave my key. No note. I had considered leaving one, but Josh didn't even deserve a goodbye.

I texted Morgan once I got into the cab to let her know I was on my way to the airport. I was two hours early for my flight, but with New York traffic I didn't want to miss my plane for any reason. Sitting at JFK for an extra hour would be better than staying in that apartment for another minute. I didn't have much, but I had enough money saved up to tide me over until I found a new job.

Six hours later, I was standing outside the Louis Armstrong Airport. The humid air caused my hair to frizz, adding to my already bedraggled look. I checked my phone: nothing. Josh wouldn't notice I was gone for a few hours yet. I texted Morgan when my plane landed, but she hadn't responded. I assumed that meant she was on her way; she was a stickler for phone usage while driving. Looking around, I saw a man with a bouquet hugging a woman who had just arrived as well and thought of Josh again. He used to buy me flowers and small trinkets from time to time. *Stop that. He was human garbage,* I reminded myself. I had traveled by myself once to attend the funeral of a great-aunt. He was supposed to meet me at the airport when I returned, but when I got there all I got was a text saying he got caught up at work. "Take an Uber," he said.

"Charlieeee!" *Morgan.*

I turned and saw her hanging out the driver's window of a white Honda Accord. My eyes immediately stung, threatening me with tears. I let them come. Morgan put her hazards on and ditched her car by the sidewalk, running toward me. She wrapped me in a tight hug. I was grateful because my body wanted nothing but to sink to my knees right then and there. I was so calm and collected about this drastic life change up until this moment and reality finally caught up with me. I was at rock bottom and here was my beautiful friend riding in to rescue me in a 4-cylinder white horse.

"Girl, everything is going to be fine. I got you!" she said into my ear so fiercely as we hugged... I had to laugh. My laugh, of course, came out as a strangled sob. She grabbed one of my bags as I wiped tears and snot on my sleeve.

I ogled the city as she drove to her place. She chattered non-stop about everything she'd been up to since we graduated and went separate ways. When we got to her apartment, I was surprised. We'd stayed in touch mostly through social media throughout the years, and I knew she was doing well with her job in marketing, but she downplayed her success. She lived in the French Quarter. Her building was beautiful and had a doorman, Harvey, who greeted her by name. Coming from New York City, I didn't exactly expect to be "starstruck" by New Orleans... but I was.

Inside her apartment, we were greeted by her French bulldog, Jean-Claude. His sturdy little body wriggled with excitement over a new visitor. Morgan showed me to my room so I could freshen up before we went back out for dinner. We ended up going to a place called Meauxbar, a few blocks from Morgan's apartment. The food was divine. I've always enjoyed French cooking, but the cajun flair to the food was like nothing I'd ever experienced before. Morgan was respectful of my situation and kept the conversation light as we ate. After our meal, we stayed for a few drinks.

"So, I'm so glad to see you again, don't get me wrong," Morgan started. I could see she was feeling a little looser, thanks to Meauxbar's hibiscus tequila cocktails. "But you didn't give me much information before showing up. What the hell happened? I thought you had the perfect life! Don't get me wrong, I am *so* happy you're here. Jean-Claude and I were getting lonely in that place." My phone buzzed angrily in my purse. I silenced it and glanced at Morgan to see if she noticed. She did.

"It's been a long time coming," I scoffed, the alcohol giving my sad story a touch of sass. "At first, yeah, things were great with Josh." I avoided her eyes and took another sip. "But I found out Josh had a few female coworkers that he had a habit of getting drinks with... too often. I'm not really the jealous type, but coming home at 4:00 A.M on a weeknight kind of left me with some questions." Morgan nodded knowingly. She'd known Josh first. She was the one who introduced us. "At first I thought it was just a fluke," I continued. "But when it happened more often, I started asking him about it. He never admitted to anything, *of course*, but when he reacted to my questions physically instead of just answering... I figured it out for myself." My hand moved to my cheek. I shrugged and silenced my phone for a second time. Morgan's brow furrowed with concern.

"Damn," she said after a moment. "Damn, that boy. Damn. That. *Boy*," she emphasized, raising her voice a little. "Seven years together to end like that." She shook her head, tossing her dark curls. "I'm so sorry. But... I am glad that you're here with me, right now. Honestly." She grabbed my hand and stared into my eyes. She was more drunk than me, but her eyes were bright. Despite the upheaval of life as I knew it, I felt good. It gave me hope that I could come back from this. I could do it.

We stumbled home a few hours later, her arm over my shoulder. Harvey let us in with a harmless but knowing smirk. She gave me a glass of water before I retreated to my room for the night. It's funny. I was always the more responsible one when we were in college. Now she's taking care of me. I brushed my teeth carelessly and flopped into my new bed, too exhausted to undress. Now that I had some privacy, I decided to look at my phone. I had 7 missed calls, 2 voicemails, and 33 texts from Josh. I listened to the voicemails and deleted them as I went. I read through the texts, the last one sent at 1:17 AM. Reading them was like watching a slow descent into madness as Josh got more frustrated and angered by my lack of response. I had to speak to him eventually... but not today.

I woke the next morning to the smell of coffee, pancakes, and bacon. Warm sunlight spilled through the gossamer curtains into my room. I smiled. It felt like I was on vacation. Morgan smiled at me as I entered the kitchen.

"A bit different from our college days," she said. "I guess you could say I got a bit bougie about brunch." She winked at me as she handed me a cup of coffee.

"Thanks," I said as I took the mug from her. She transferred some sizzling bacon to a plate covered with paper towels. Jean-Claude sneezed at her feet, reminding her of his presence in hopes he might get a snack. When Morgan ignored him, he came to me, begging with his round eyes. "Can I give him a piece?" I asked, gesturing to the bacon. Morgan shrugged and replied that it was fine if I only gave him a little bite. Jean-Claude and I were quickly becoming best friends.

"So, what are your plans? What's your next move?" Morgan asked, gripping her mug and leaning on her counter. I faltered.

"I don't really know... start looking for a job, I guess. I'll probably start sending out some resumes after breakfast..." *And maybe talk to Josh.*

"That can wait until Monday," Morgan interrupted. "It's the weekend and I haven't seen you in years!"

About seven years, if I recall correctly, I thought guiltily. I knew she was into Josh when she introduced us. I made a mental note to discuss this with her, maybe after a few drinks later in the day.

"I think we should go out tonight," Morgan went on. "I'll show you around New Orleans, get you established." I reluctantly agreed. I wanted to send some feelers out for the job market as soon as possible. I didn't know how long it would take before I got a job, and I surely didn't want my welcome to wear out before then.

"Do you have anything cute to wear?" Morgan asked. Admittedly, I did not. When I packed I just grabbed the bare essentials.

"Uh... I have jeans and a few nice shirts, I guess." I shrugged. Morgan laughed.

"You're gonna wear jeans in this heat? With what, an old Sublime t-shirt? Nah. There's this cute little consignment shop two blocks from here. I'd go with you, but I have to meet with a client I was supposed to see yesterday. I'll be quick, an hour tops. You can take Jean-Claude with you, if you want!" Jean-Claude looked up from my feet at the sound of his name. "Or," she added, seeing the look of uncertainty on my face, "You can hang out here and send out applications and I'll take you there when I get back." It had just dawned on me that she must have taken a half day at her job yesterday in order to pick me up at the airport. I felt guilty and humbled that after all this time she was still such a great friend to me.

"I'll send a few out and then go. No need for both of us to stay cooped up on a beautiful day like this!" I said, gesturing out her glass balcony doors. Morgan smiled.

"Great! I'll leave a spare key fob for you to get back inside," she said, excited.

After breakfast was cleaned up, Morgan placed the key fob on the counter for me and ducked out. I hadn't had a job for the past 4 years. Josh insisted on supporting the two of us. Just another way for him to control me. I would have to work hard to build my resume up to land a "real" job. After sending out a few applications for retail jobs, I typed up a quick text to Josh. I did my best to sound detached and absolute. I let him know that I was safe, and that I never wanted to see or speak with him again. Satisfied with my message, I sent the text, then decided to take Jean-Claude for a walk.

We strolled the streets of New Orleans together. A local dog as my tour guide and me; a stranger to everyone I passed on the sidewalk. I spotted the boutique consignment store that Morgan mentioned earlier, nestled between a florist and a small convenience store. I stopped in the convenience store to grab a few toiletries that I had forgotten to pack and then went next door to the consignment. The shop smelled like old fabrics and various herbs, but was still clean and tidy. The elderly woman who worked there side-eyed Jean-Claude when she approached me, but didn't complain about his presence in the store.

"Can I help you find something?" she asked with a southern drawl. I couldn't help but marvel at her accent. She must've noticed the fascination on my face, either that, or the bruising on my cheekbone that was still sore and slightly visible. "You're not from here, are you?" She continued. I smiled sheepishly.

"It's that noticeable, huh? I, uh… I actually just got here yesterday, from New York. I was looking for something a little lighter to wear… maybe a nice sundress?" The woman eyed me up and down again before replying.

"You're in the right spot," she said, pointing at the rack of dresses I had been poking through. "But—" She paused for a moment. "I think I have a dress that will be *perfect* for you. I'll be right back." She turned and walked through the double doors marked "Employees Only." When she returned, she was holding a beautiful dress. It was simple, but far from boring. Elegant and yet coquettish. It was white linen with small blue roses accenting the neckline. "I had to repair this strap," the woman said, running her fingers along the left shoulder. "It's as good as new now." I took the dress from her and held it against myself. The fabric was so soft and light, not at all what I was expecting. It looked and felt like it was made for me. I was sold. I selected a few tank tops and pairs of shorts as well before heading to the register to check out.

"It's a beautiful city," the woman said as she folded the clothing to place into a plastic bag. "But don't let the beauty fool you. It has a lot of history; good and bad. You be careful and mind your surroundings while you visit."

"Oh, I'm not just visiting... I plan to stay for a little while." I said, trying to sound more confident than I was about my circumstances. She smiled at me, but her eyes looked sad. My phone buzzed in my pocket. A text. *From Josh?*

"Well, in that case, welcome home, young lady." She spoke gently. "I hope whatever you're running from doesn't catch up with you. Take care of yourself, child." She turned and disappeared through the double doors. I stood there for a moment, trying to figure out what to make of her. Or of myself. Was I that much of an open book? A gentle tug from Jean-Claude's leash pulled me out of my thoughts. I looked at my phone. The text was from Morgan, saying she would be home soon.

A thousand thoughts swam through my mind as we strolled back to Morgan's building. I pictured the old woman from the store as some kind of hoodoo or voodoo conjurer, reading my thoughts and my past and maybe even my future... and I had to laugh. I know that New Orleans locals can be superstitious, but I felt silly for jumping on the bandwagon so soon after my arrival. I could see Morgan's building up ahead. My phone buzzed and I looked, expecting Morgan. When I saw it was Josh calling, my heart went to my throat. I took a deep breath to calm my nerves before answering.

"Hello?"

"Where the fuck are you?" Josh's voice was ragged.

"I'm with my family," I lied, badly. He didn't need to know where I was.

"Liar," he snarled. "You haven't spoken to your parents in years. Who are you with?"

"That's none of your business anymore," I replied curtly, but my voice was shaking. "I told you. We're finished. There's nothing more to say."

"You think you can just disappear to New Orleans and start fresh just like that?" Josh asked. I froze. How did he know where I was? "I saw your emails. Plane ticket confirmation and some sad job applications? Hah. Good luck with that." I made a mental note to change all my passwords, hating myself for being so stupid, hating Josh for being an asshole. I saw Morgan coming from the opposite direction, as did Jean-Claude. He started yapping and caught her attention. I needed to end this phone call quickly.

"Listen, Josh, I'm gone and there's nothing you can do to get me back, so why don't you just leave me the fuck alone," I spat out, heat rising in my face as the words spilled from my mouth. "You don't get to hit me and then get angry when I leave. Do *not* contact me again." I hung up just as Morgan approached.

"Hey..." she said, eyeing my face cautiously. "You ok? Was that him?" I nodded, focusing on my breathing before trying to speak. Morgan took Jean-Claude's leash from my hand and saw the plastic bag in the other. "You found the place! Did you get anything good?" I was grateful for the change of subject. While we walked into her apartment building, I calmed down enough to speak at a normal volume and pitch. "Remind me to change all my passwords when we get inside."

I didn't need her to remind me. As soon as we got into the apartment, I opened my laptop and set to work on changing passwords and privacy settings. It was tedious, especially with my phone connected to so many accounts as well. Did he track my phone before I changed the password? I felt uneasy about the idea of him knowing exactly where I was in the city. After I was certain all my login information had been changed, I let out a sigh of relief and closed my laptop.

"He might know where I am... where you live." I shot a worried glance at Morgan. "I'm not sure if he tracked my phone to this location, but apparently, he knows I'm somewhere in this city."

Morgan looked contemplative. "I wouldn't worry about it. Even if he was crazy enough to fly down here, Harvey would never let him into the building without permission."

Josh might not be allowed inside, I thought, *but that won't keep me safe after I leave the building.*

After Morgan pressed again to see what I bought at the consignment, I retreated into my bedroom to try on the new dress. The moment my hands touched it I felt a rush of excitement and energy. The dress felt cool to the touch, as if it had just been taken out of a refrigerator. It had just enough material and support that I could even wear it without a bra. The feel of the fabric against my skin was incredible. I felt beautiful and empowered as I gazed upon my reflection in the mirror. Even my hair looked smoother and glossier than it had minutes ago, my skin seemed to be glowing. The bruise on my cheek barely ached any longer. I felt... unstoppable. Confident in my new outfit, I returned to the living room to show Morgan.

The look on her face when she saw the dress cut my confidence in half. Somewhat deflated, I raised my hands. "What's wrong?" I asked. Morgan shrugged and shook her head.

"Nothing, I mean if you like that dress, I guess it's cool..." she deflected. "It just kind of looks old and frumpy to me." I gaped at her. Was she looking at the same dress? I turned back to the mirror in my room. The dress was beautiful. *I* was beautiful in it. Oh well, at least I wouldn't have to worry about her wanting to borrow it. I loved this dress. I turned back to Morgan.

"So, where are we going?" I asked.

We spent the afternoon visiting the major touristy areas, stopping occasionally for a mimosa or two. I felt more than a few pairs of eyes follow me throughout the day, but instead of feelings of paranoia, I felt elated. I felt like a celebrity. I took pictures with Morgan and posted them on my Instagram account, fully knowing Josh would probably see them and become jealous. He already knew where I was at that point, and I wanted him to see how much fun I was having without him.

Sure enough, less than 15 minutes after posting I received an angry text from him.

"Glad to see you're having so much fun with Morgan. Enjoy being a slut in NOLA, I'll be here waiting for you to come crawling back when she gets tired of you sleeping on her couch."

I showed the text to Morgan, and we threw our heads back and laughed. Raising my glass to my lips, I made eye contact with an older man sitting a few tables away. Our haughty laughter must have caught his attention. I held my gaze as I took a sip, licking traces of the mimosa from my upper lip afterward. The man stared for a moment before dropping eye contact to bury his face behind his phone, his ears turning bright red. Morgan noticed the exchange and playfully hit my arm, but in doing so, she spilled her Kir Royale onto the table. I watched in horror as the bright pink beverage splashed onto my new dress, but to my amazement, the liquid beaded up and rolled off onto the floor.

"Damn, that was lucky," she said as we sopped the remaining liquid off the table with our napkins.

Afterward, Morgan and I walked around in the Jazz Museum before making our way to *Les Marées Changeantes*, a French restaurant and bar for dinner. There was a live band setting up as we were seated. As we ate and ordered drink after drink, I found myself watching the bassist. I also found him watching me.

"Should I send him a drink?" I asked Morgan, who wore a smug and amused face. "What do you think he drinks?"

"Why don't you ask him yourself?" Morgan winked at me as she stood up from the table. "I'll be back in a few..." I watched her head to the bathroom and was surprised by a tap on my shoulder a moment later.

"You having a good time, yeah?" The bassist stood beside me at our table. His accent was not as thick as the woman from the consignment shop, but still noticeable. I nodded and smiled.

"Actually, I was just trying to figure out what kind of drink I could buy you," I said, gesturing to the empty seat at the table. He sat, raising the glass of water he held in his hand. "I appreciate the offer, *cher*, but I don't drink. Too many wild nights for this one. My name is Rene."

"My name is Charlie," I replied. Rene raised his eyebrows and grinned. "Like Charlie Parker! You're in the right town with a name like that. Are you a jazz fan?" he asked. "Love it, I'm a huge fan." I lied. I don't think I've ever intentionally listened to jazz music before and had no idea who Charlie Parker was.

"Do you have any plans for after the show?" I asked, trying to quickly change the subject.

"We've got another 20 minutes left in our set if you want to stick around," he said, eyes twinkling. "That could be arranged," I replied coyly, relieved he didn't ask who my favorite musicians were.

Morgan emerged from the restrooms and made a detour to the bar when she noticed Rene sitting with me. I returned my gaze to him as he finished his water. "I better get back to my spot, but it was great meeting you. I do hope you stay to chat more after," he said with a kind smile. When he stood up to leave, I grasped his hand and stood as well, giving him a quick kiss on the cheek. He looked at me with surprise, but his expression softened and he smiled again. He kissed the back of my hand and said he'd see me soon before heading back to the small stage.

Morgan immediately returned to the table, having seen the interaction. "What the hell was that? Where did that come from?" she asked in astonishment. I laughed. "I have no idea, honestly. It was just like an impulse... it just happened." My face flushed a bit, and I smoothed out the skirt of my dress on my lap, shocked and a little embarrassed at my own behavior. I looked over to where Rene stood with his bandmates, fiddling with the tuning pegs on his instrument. He smiled at me once more when he saw I was looking.

"Damn, Charlie. You sure ain't wasting any time getting over Josh." Morgan laughed and clinked glasses with me. I waved my hand at her with a dismissive flick. "I'm just having a little fun... it *is* the weekend like you said."

By the time the band had finished playing their last song, Morgan and I had completed another round of margaritas. Rene waved at us and gave us the "be there in one minute" gesture. That was when my phone buzzed with a single-sentence text from Josh. My blood turned to ice when I read what it said.

"Who is that guy?"

I paled, looking around the room, frantically searching for his face in the crowd, but couldn't find anyone resembling him. Standing up abruptly, I showed the text to Morgan and said we needed to leave. As we rushed out the door, I shot an apologetic glance over my shoulder at Rene, who stood there looking confused. When we got back to Morgan's apartment, I told her I was exhausted and just wanted to go to bed. While in reality, my heart was still racing at the idea that Josh was somehow at the bar, watching me.

The next morning was rough. It felt like I had been hit by a truck, which is what I deserve for day drinking and gallivanting around in the heat and humidity. Between feverish gulps of water, I slowly began to feel a little better. I entered the living room to see Morgan on her phone. She put it face down on the table when she noticed me.

"How're you feeling this morning? Coffee's in the pot and I've got some aspirin in the bathroom if you need any." Morgan chuckled into her coffee. "Yeah, that sounds pretty good," I responded groggily. Morgan's phone buzzed, but she didn't look at it.

"You going to answer that...?" I asked. I was all too familiar with phones placed facedown, something Josh would do constantly when exchanging messages with his "co-workers" at all hours of the day. Morgan shrugged dismissively and replied that it wasn't important. Taking a mental note, I became more intrigued and decided to prod further. "How do you think Josh knew I was talking to that guy last night?"

Morgan rolled her eyes. "He probably just assumed you were out and talking to guys, especially after you posted those pictures of us. It's what cheaters do; they project their own shitty behaviors onto others." Her voice wasn't harsh, but it still had a slight edge to it.

"I guess that's a possibility... it just made me a little nervous to think he might have followed me here." I was careful with my next words. "... Or that he might have someone else here to keep tabs on me, you know?" Morgan's phone buzzed again.

I then retreated back to my room, telling Morgan that I wanted to take a shower, but suspicion and paranoia were already tracing their cold fingers through my mind. *Was she lying to me?* When I emerged from the bathroom, the apartment was empty except for Jean-Claude. I was about to try on one of the other outfits I purchased, but then I noticed the dress. It was laid out perfectly on the bed, looking beautiful as ever. I know when I took it off last night, I left it crumpled on the floor, but now it looked like it had just been freshly dry-cleaned.

The second my hand touched it, my lingering headache disappeared almost instantly. I picked it up to examine it and noticed something I had missed before. When the woman from the consignment shop brought it out to me, she told me that she had just repaired the left shoulder strap, but I couldn't see any fresh stitching or signs of repairs anywhere on the garment. I put the dress back on and was once again infatuated with how it felt and how it fit my body... like it was made just for me.

I heard the door and the pitter-patter of Jean-Claude's feet on the hardwood floor. Morgan stood in the kitchen, placing grocery bags on the counter.

"Hey, I just ran out to grab some food and snacks. I figured we could stay in tonight and watch some cheesy—" She stopped when she saw me in my bedroom doorway. "Wearing that dress again? I thought you bought other stuff too." I only shrugged in response. "Speaking of which," Morgan continued. "Where exactly did you find the thrift store you bought that dress from? I usually walk past it when I go food shopping, but it wasn't there anymore."

"Who was it that you were texting this morning before you left?" I asked, ignoring her question. Morgan looked taken aback. "That's really none of your business, honestly. I have my own personal life too," she responded defensively.

"I just think it's kind of funny that you left to go to the bathroom last night and not long after is when I got that text from Josh. That's all. Oh, and did you touch my dress? It wasn't where I left it."

"If you *must* know," Morgan was getting frustrated, but I didn't care. "I was texting a friend of mine who is a cop here. I was asking about if you might be able to file a restraining order against Josh or something because of that creepy text. Just in case things escalated. I didn't tell you this morning because you'd just woken up and looked like hell. Also, no, I didn't touch your stupid dress. You're acting a bit obsessive over it, to be honest."

I glared at her a moment, assessing her body language, then sighed. "I need some fresh air," I said, brushing past her. I grabbed my things and the spare key fob and went out the door before she could respond.

Once outside, I started to feel better, but something that she said was still nagging me. I retraced my steps from my first day, looking for the thrift store I'd bought the dress from. To my surprise, I passed the flower shop and next to it stood... a tourist shop? The display window was full of "I ♥ NOLA" t-shirts and trinkets. On the other side was the convenience store. I looked up and down the street, wondering if I had been confused, but everything else looked exactly the same as it did before. I must have looked a bit lost and confused (because I *was*) and a young man approached me asking if I needed help. I politely declined and attempted to continue walking when he grabbed my wrist and said he could take me wherever I needed to go.

I whirled on him and gripped his forearm tightly. "If you touch me again I will break each of your fingers!" I snarled at him. His eyes widened in shock, and he released his grip instantly, holding his hands up as if I had him at gunpoint.

"I'm sorry, ma'am, I was only trying to help." He managed to say, before making a hasty retreat. *Well, that was interesting.* I had never really stood up for myself like that before. At least, not in such an aggressive way. It felt good.

By the time I came back to Morgan's apartment, it was nearing dark. Morgan left a note on the counter for me to let me know she was sorry if she made things uncomfortable earlier and that she had gone out with a friend and would be back later if I still wanted to have a movie night with her. I must have dozed off, because it was completely dark outside when I woke up.

"What are you doing, Charlie?" Morgan's voice cut through the silence. I glanced around and saw that I was standing at the windows overlooking the city. "Charlie!" Morgan repeated. I turned to see her standing in the kitchen, looking bewildered.

"What?" I asked.

"You were just standing there muttering to yourself in the darkness when I came in. I tried texting and calling you to let you know I was on my way home and you never responded. Then it took me several tries to get you to snap out of it just now. It was really creepy." Morgan explained.

"I don't know what you're talking about, I just came home and took a nap." I responded sharply. "By the way... who were you out with? Was it Josh? Is he here?"

Morgan looked at me incredulously. "What? No! Why would I meet with him or even talk to him after what he did to you?"

I smirked and approached her in the kitchen. "I know you had a thing for him back in college when you introduced us. Don't deny it," I spoke calmly and evenly. "You couldn't wait to scoop him up after I left him, and you've been the one texting him. You were always jealous that he chose me over you."

"What? Charlie—that's crazy. I would never! What's gotten into you?" Morgan sputtered. "You've been acting so differently ever since you bought that weird dress. I mean, you've been wearing it for two straight days now!"

"So you admit, you just want me to take it off so you can try to steal that too?" I continued to get closer. Morgan was looking even more uneasy. She knew I was right in my accusations.

"Charlie, whatever is going on, I can't help but think that it has something to do with the dress. You have to destroy it, it's changing you. You're not the same when you wear it!"

My hand found the large chef knife sitting on the drying rack next to the sink as I crept closer and Morgan retreated. Jean-Claude began to bark.

Astonishingly, blood doesn't stain this dress either. The droplets rolled off as if the fabric was coated in a hydrophobic material. However, I still needed to take a shower to remove Morgan's blood from my hair, face, and arms. The quick shower felt agonizingly long, as I left the dress on my bed, but once I was cleaned up and had the dress back on, all was right again. Gathering my things and heading for the door, I walked past Jean-Claude's food and water bowls. I glanced around the apartment and saw him crouched underneath the coffee table. When I approached him with his leash, he flinched away from me when I reached for him, but I was quicker. I grabbed a few of his items and stuffed them into my backpack and carried him out with me. Harvey greeted me politely as I left the building and hailed a cab.

Just as I reached my gate, I could hear the announcement that boarding for the flight to JFK was about to begin. I approached the counter and handed the airline personnel my boarding pass. Once we were situated on the plane, I took him out and placed him on my lap to offer him some water. A flight attendant stopped by.

"Aw, what a cute little pup! He's so well-behaved." She cooed. "What's his name?

"Thanks," I replied cooly, "His name is Jean-Claude and this is his first flight, so he's a bit nervous."

"That's adorable. Just so you know, he has to go back into his carrier for takeoff and landing. Do you two have big plans for New York?" She inquired politely.

"Yeah, actually, this is going to be a surprise visit for my boyfriend, Josh." I smiled back.

GOOD BOY

B EAR IS A GOOD boy. He greets his people with a wagging
tail every day when they return from outside. Sometimes, his
people call him a "bad dog." Like when he eats food that's not his,
or when he treats himself to a mud bath to cool off in the summer.
Deep down though, Bear knows that he is a good boy.

He waits patiently by the front door, watching the car pull into
the drive. His tail thumps loudly against the wall when he sees them
get out of the car. He knows he mustn't jump up to lick their faces
when they come through the door, so he stomps his feet to release
the energy. A weathered hand pats him on the head.

"Good boy, Bear," Joe says. Joe is Bear's man. He brought Bear
home many years ago to his mate, Sheila. Bear liked her too, but she
had a shorter temper than Joe did.

They shuffled past him, smelling of delicious foods, to go sit on
the couch. Bear knew this was their routine, but was always a little
disappointed that they rarely ever brought any food home to share
with him. He lay quietly by Joe's feet as he read his book. The TV
was tuned in to some nightly news, babbling away. Sheila sat in the
big chair, tying knots in a string with her sticks. Bear knew from
long ago never to chew on those particular sticks, but the ball of

string always tempted him. When he was a puppy, he used to dig into the basket where she kept them and have himself a great time. He learned that he was a "bad dog" on those days.

"Well, that is just awful!" Sheila said at one point, jerking Joe out of the book he was reading.

"Huh, what's that?" he asked. Her eyes were on the TV.

"They just said there was a family down in Florida that was killed in their home. A husband and wife and a sweet little girl. They were about to go on vacation, so nobody came looking for them right away." She put her hand to her throat.

Joe grunted. "Oh yes, that is awful," he said agreeably. He tried not to get caught up in the news stories like that. He saw no sense in getting all twisted up over the evils of the world, but Sheila sought them out. He went back to reading as the news switched to a story about a children's library opening.

After some time, Joe closed his book and took his glasses off to rub his eyes. Bear put his head on his lap and nudged his free hand. It was time to go outside. Bear burst through the back door when Joe opened it and did his business in the woods. It was a nice warm night, so Bear took his time sniffing around and remarking any shrubs and trees that needed a refresher.

Something strange struck his nose near the side of the house. A new-person smell. Bear had met a lot of Joe and Sheila's friends and remembered their scents. He even remembered the mailman and the person who came to mow the lawn. He tried to find more traces, but Joe was whistling for him to come back inside. Bear snuffed a few times to store the scent in his memory and returned to the back door.

After his people went to bed, Bear went back downstairs to sleep on the couch. He wasn't allowed on the couch, so he always moved to his rug before they came down in the morning.

He woke with a start when he heard something and immediately jumped off the couch, worried that he had been caught. But it was still dark in the house, still night time. Bear stretched and yawned in relief and made his way over to his water bowl. He stopped when he saw the outline of a person standing in the window. It was still dark, and Bear's eyes weren't as good as they used to be, so he just froze and stared, uncertain if the shadows were playing tricks on him.

Bear's fur was just standing up when the figure moved. He ran to the window, barking madly. He did not like this person standing there like that. It ran off quickly into the night after he barked. Bear stared out the window for a while, before going to check other windows. Satisfied when he saw no other suspicious figures, he fell asleep by the front door.

The next morning when Bear was let outside, he went straight to the spot outside the window where he saw the shadow person. The smell was the exact same one he had noticed before bed. It was much stronger and pungent this time. Certain smells were brought out more when accompanied by the smell of fear. Bear wagged his tail at that. Bear was a good boy.

Julia was busy helping a customer pick out a harness for their new puppy when she saw the man walk into the store. She helped them fit the harness for the wiggling mop of hair at their feet. Once the harness was snug, she clipped the leash on and quickly demonstrated how to use it. She always thought it was funny when people used anti-pull harnesses on small breeds, but the customer seemed satisfied enough. She was sorting through the mess of tried-and-failed harnesses that the owner had pulled off the racks when the man approached her.

"Excuse me," he said in a soft, timid voice. "Can you help me pick out some dog treats?"

Julia was glad to abandon the tangled mess of harnesses, if only temporarily. "Sure! What are you looking for? There are different kinds of treats for different purposes."

The man smiled; he seemed uncomfortable. "Ah, well, I'm not quite sure. Something for a big dog, maybe?" Julia motioned for him to follow as she led him to the dog treat section.

"What breed of dog?" she asked, over her shoulder.

"It's not my dog, so I don't really know. It's a friend's dog that I think I might need some help winning over."

"I see," Julia smiled at him, "well, we have some antlers over here that will last a long time and dogs love them." She grabbed a bag off the shelf. "But these soft treats are good for training if it's something that's going to take a little more time. How much time do plan to spend at your friend's house?"

"It's open-ended, at this point. At least a few days," the man said. His eyes glanced over the assortment of treats on the shelf, rarely making contact with Julia's. Something about the way he was acting made her a little uncomfortable, but she couldn't tell what exactly it was about him that made her feel that way.

"Ok well, you let me know if there's anything else I can help you with," she said in her best customer service voice. She brushed off the man's strangeness as social awkwardness and returned to the mess in the harness aisle.

When Bear was let out that night before his people went to bed, he discovered something delightful. Hidden around the yard were small treats! Bear found five and was convinced there were more when Joe called him back. Reluctantly he came inside, stopping twice to recheck spots he had previously found a treat hidden.

Bear fell asleep so fast that night, he felt like a puppy. Play hard, sleep hard. He was pulled from his deep sleep when he heard someone walking around on the wooden floors. It was still dark, too early for Joe or Sheila to be up and about. Groggily, Bear got to his feet. He padded up the carpeted stairs to check on them. Their room smelled funny when he nosed his way past the door. Something was wrong. The room stank of something Bear was unfamiliar with. It still smelled like his people, but different somehow. Bear put his front paws on Joe's side of the bed and nudged him with his nose. Joe was dead. Next to him, Sheila had a pillow over her face, but all Bear could smell was death.

Then Bear heard a noise down the hallway and realized he smelled another person mixed with Joe and Sheila's scents. Bear was quiet as he made his way down the hall, the stench of the stranger filling his mouth and nose. His black fur helped him creep along the shadows. When he saw the man rummaging through Joe's things, he let out a low growl. The man froze and slowly turned.

"H-hey, puppy." His voice was uncertain. The smell of fear coming off of him in waves was almost intoxicating to Bear.

The man reached into a pocket. "You're a good boy, right? Be a good boy." Bear continued to growl but stepped back. Bear *was* a good boy. He had never bitten a person before, but for the first time in his life, he had an irresistible urge to do just that. Would that make him a bad dog? The man held a treat and tossed it to him. It was just like those treats he found in the yard. He sniffed it cautiously, not taking his eyes off the man. The man stepped forward and Bear barked loudly as a warning. Reaching into his pocket again, he produced a long object. He held it out for Bear to sniff at.

Back down the hall, Sheila took a big gulp of air as she regained consciousness. She fumbled for the phone beside the bed but knocked it to the floor. She heard Bear barking aggressively somewhere in the house. She coughed and called out weakly.

"Bear!"

Bear's head was turned, listening to the sounds coming from his people's bedroom, when the man moved abruptly. He hit Bear on the head with the object he had been holding. Bear was no longer concerned with being a good boy. He saw red and crunched down hard on the man's leg. The shrieks of pain seemed to suddenly unleash some primal instinct in Bear he never knew he had. He bit down hard and shook his head back and forth. He felt the soft flesh tear between his teeth, oblivious to the blows landing on his head. He let go only to latch on to one of the hands beating on him. The man's howls of pain rose in pitch as Bear crunched through two of the fingers.

Sheila screamed in the other room and that snapped Bear out of his frenzy. He turned and ran from the bloodied man to her, feeling a little guilty. Perhaps he was a bad dog for biting a person. Sheila was leaning over Joe, shaking him and crying for him to come back. Bear knew he shouldn't, but he jumped onto the bed to comfort her. Sheila pushed him away until she realized her hand had blood on it where she touched Bear. She looked at him. His graying muzzle was stained crimson. The sight of him seemed to snap her back into the reality of the situation they were in, and she grabbed the phone and called the police.

Bear had returned to guard the man after he knew that Sheila was okay, but the man was gone. He tracked the blood and scent back downstairs and out the back door. He wagged his tail a little, proud of himself for scaring that man away. When the cops finally arrived, Bear had to be put away in the garage. He wouldn't let more strange men into the house. One of them came in to check on him and make sure he wasn't hurt, but had to make a hasty retreat when Bear lunged at the door. Hours later, Bear calmed down and was looked at by an EMT.

"He seems to be fine. I don't think any of that blood is his," he told the police. The forensics tech took swabs of blood from Bear's muzzle and bagged them up for analysis to make sure they matched the blood found in the upstairs study. They let Sheila know what objects from the room they would need to collect for evidence. She barely even glanced at them, still in shock. She picked up one of the evidence bags. Inside it was a blood-stained antler piece.

"Is this... is this from the deer head on the wall?" she asked.

The policemen exchanged glances. "No ma'am, this was on the floor. We assumed it belonged to the dog."

Sheila shook her head. "No, we've never bought any antlers for Bear."

Jesse was finishing his double shift in the ER when the man limped through the doors. His hand was wrapped in a blood-soaked rag. One of the new nurses, Ellen, Jesse remembered, rushed over to him and asked him questions as she found a wheelchair for him to sit in. It irritated Jesse because she had left her position at the patient-intake desk. He checked his watch and sighed. Twenty minutes left on his shift, but this would easily take longer. The nurse was unwrapping the man's hand when he stepped in and took over, asking her to return to her station. The man's left pinky and ring fingers were horribly mangled. The third finger looked salvageable, but the pinky would have to be removed.

"What's your name, sir?" Jesse asked as he wheeled him into a room to clean and dress the wounds.

"It's... uh, Remy." Jesse glanced sideways at him from the medical cart.

"And what happened to you?" Remy would not make eye contact. "Dog. Big dog," was all he said in response. "It got my leg too."

"I see that." Jesse had seen a lot of things over time working in the ER. "We're going to take care of your hand first, though." He bent to inspect Remy's leg. He could see the large gashes in the calf through the torn pant leg. "We'll have to administer rabies shots as well. Do you know the dog that attacked you?" Remy shook his head.

"I—I was just walking down the street and it ran out and bit me. As Jesse stood, there was a knock at the door. Ellen poked her head in.

"I'm sorry to interrupt, Doctor, but I need to speak with you." She glanced at the man, then back to Jesse.

"OK, I'll be right out," Jesse responded, irritated once more that she had left her station once yet again. He handed a fistful of gauze to the man and said, "I'll be right back. Keep pressure on that hand so you don't lose any more blood."

Ellen stood outside the room. She looked shaken. "Is everything okay?" Jesse asked, mostly out of politeness instead of genuine concern.

"I just got off the phone. Police just put out a notice to all hospitals and emergency clinics in the area." This caught Jesse's attention. "They're looking for a man with severe wounds from a dog attack. He broke into a house and was chased off by the family dog. They wouldn't tell me anything else except that this man is extremely dangerous." Jesse thought for a moment.

"I need you to contact the police right now," Jesse said calmly. "We can't be certain that this is the guy, but we'll let the police figure that out." Ellen nodded and took off.

Jesse smiled wryly. He could forget about getting home anytime soon now. Once the cops showed up, he'd be stuck answering a thousand meaningless questions and filling out statement forms. Fucking perfect way to end the day. He considered going back to the patient room to help the poor bastard with his fingers, but decided against it. He went for a coffee instead and told one of the bigger orderlies to stay outside the door. For all he knew, the guy in there could be a serial killer.

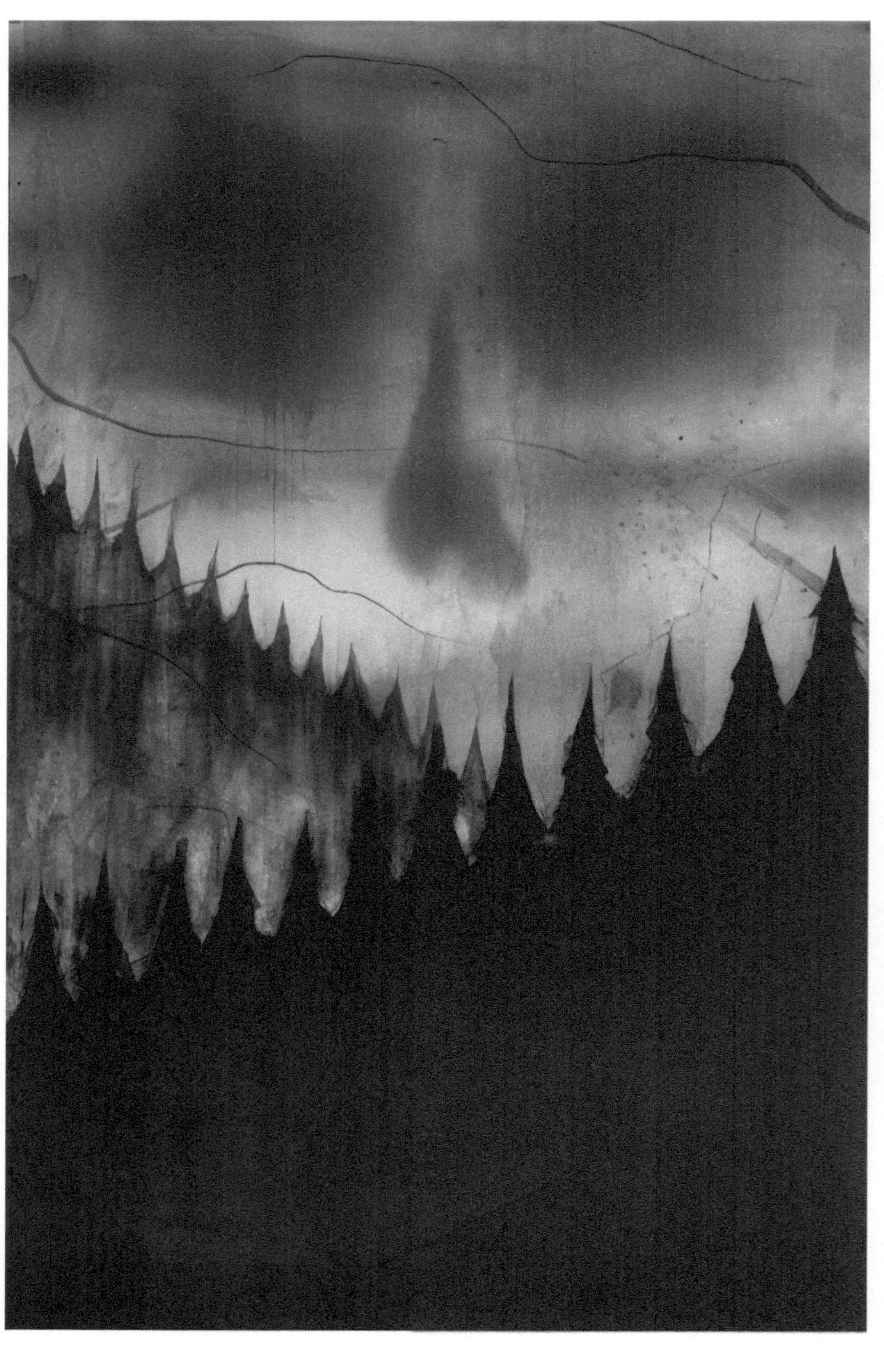

TRUST

IT WAS A RAINY week, which didn't bother Ethan. He was happy for a reprieve from the relentless heat and humidity that came with August in the south. As the last days of summer dwindled, he was determined to have one last hoorah with his friends before they scattered off to their chosen universities. The five of them had been inseparable since middle school and this sudden and inevitable change left Ethan trying not to be envious of them for branching out into the world. He had decided to attend the local community college to save his parents some money.

He was hoping the rain would let up at least a day or two before their big adventure. Ethan and his best friend Jacob had planned a camping trip one night after a few drags on a wrinkled joint. "We should get some poles and tents and hike out to Blue Ridge Lake for a weekend. You, me, Sam, Aaron, and Tommy," Jacob said excitedly between coughs.

Ethan liked the idea immediately. It was low-budget; most of the supplies they would need could be scavenged from their parents' garages. It also allowed them to spend quality time together before going separate ways the following week. Ethan knew that "quality time" was a term to be laughed at by the rest of his buddies, so he did not say those exact words out loud when suggesting the idea to them.

The sky was still cloudy the day they were packing up the supplies, but the sun was peeking through reassuringly. Ethan's father called him inside to speak with him in private. "You boys be careful this weekend," he began in a serious tone. "Blue Ridge Lake is a huge reservation, nothing but wilderness for miles." Ethan braced himself, knowing his father was about to give him the typical "be safe, make right choices" speech. But when his father produced a small black case from under the kitchen table and handed it to him, a slight chill ran down his back. His father was giving him his handgun.

"This is for emergencies only. There are a lot of wild animals out there that have learned a campsite can be an easy meal ticket." His father held on to the case and looked Ethan in the eye for a moment before releasing his grip. "Don't tell your friends you even have it with you; they'll want to see it. I trust you to be responsible with it, but I can't say the same for your friends. Especially Sam. Keep it locked up and hidden at all times."

"I will," Ethan promised solemnly. His father smiled and clapped him on the back. "I'm sure you won't even need it, but it's always better to be prepared in case you do. Have fun this weekend, kiddo."

Once the gear was loaded into Jacob's truck, the boys waved goodbye to Ethan's parents and took off down the road. On the highway, the suburban surroundings quickly disappeared and were replaced by a thick wall of towering pine trees. In this area, it didn't take long to transition from civilization to complete and utter wilderness. Ethan always liked that about where he lived. Years ago, his father would take him on fishing trips, and he would pretend they were hunter-gatherers in ancient times. It felt like they were in an alternate reality where there were no cars and large cities, only the sounds and smells of the forest and its inhabitants.

The boys took their exit and said goodbye to the highway, modern plumbing, and decent cell phone signals. Ethan couldn't help but feel a little giddy as they finally pulled into the parking lot of the campground office. As often as he had gone camping with his father, this was the first time he and his friends went completely on their own. He and Jacob went into the office to check in.

The walls of the office were filled with maps of the park and a few poorly executed taxidermy animals. One of them was a brown rabbit with antlers attached to its head behind the ears. The placard underneath read "The Elusive Jackalope," which made Ethan smile.

"Hello, boys, what can I do you for?" The elderly man behind the front desk smiled at them. He looked like a seasoned outdoorsman, with unkempt hair and a strong jawline grizzled with silver stubble.

"Just checking in for the weekend," Jacob responded politely.

"Ah," the man said as he pulled out a massive binder. He set it on the desk and paged through it. "Last name?"

"Connelly."

"I see. Well, boys, it looks like you're in luck. The rains didn't hit us too hard here in the mountains, so it shouldn't be too muddy." The man stared at the boys for a moment before adding "I'm sure you boys don't need me to remind you that alcoholic beverages, fireworks, and firearms are not permitted in the park?" Ethan immediately thought of his father's gun tucked away in his duffel bag.

"Of course not, sir," Jacob replied coolly. "We're just here to catch some fish and get some fresh air." His answer seemed to satisfy the old man. Jacob signed his name in the binder and the man handed him a folded map of the main trails.

"You can drive your car along this road here until you hit a fork, go left. Follow that until you hit the parking area. Make sure you lock everything up before you continue down this trail," he circled the trail with a red pen. "After that, you can hike until you find a decent area to set up camp. Mind you, the closer you stay to the parking area the more foot traffic you're gonna get with other campers. Not that there are many campers left out there, this late in the season. Everybody is heading back to work and school." Ethan and Jacob thanked the man and made their way back to the truck where Sam was having a smoke.

"All set?" Sam asked, stamping his cigarette butt into the ground. They got back into the truck and headed down the dirt road to the parking area. There were only a handful of cars there. A couple unpacking their Subaru waved to the boys as they rolled by. Another family was packing their camping supplies back into their Escalade, preparing to head back into civilization.

As the boys unloaded the truck, Ethan opened his duffel to store his phone in an inside pocket. The gun case poked out of the top briefly and caught Sam's eye before Ethan closed the bag up again.

"Hey, what's that?" he asked. Ethan pretended not to hear his question and slung his bag over his shoulder.

"We should get a move on, guys. I don't feel like sleeping under the stars tonight." Once they were all ready to go, the boys set out on the trail. They passed by two campsites that looked well-worn, but Sam insisted they go deeper into the woods for a better spot. After walking about thirty minutes, they passed the couple who waved to them in the parking area. The two waved cheerfully again as they struggled to pitch their tent in the small clearing.

They walked on for almost three hours until the trail they followed looked almost as if nature had taken it back, if not for the occasional markings on the trees. Finally, they came to rest in a clearing and decided that was the spot. It was large enough to accommodate the two tents and had a small fire pit lined with stones. A narrow footpath would take them down to the lake. Aaron and Tommy, who were identical twins, immediately went to work on the family-sized tent they brought.

Ethan and Jacob set up the smaller tent while Sam took off down the footpath to gather firewood. One of the cords used to secure the rain cover was twisted into a horrible knot. Ethan tried to pick at it, unsuccessfully. Frustrated, he tossed the tangled mess to the side. Tommy came over and pulled out his pocketknife.

"Want me to give it a try?"

Ethan shrugged in response. "It's no use to us as is, go for it."

Tommy cut one section of the cord with a deft flick of the blade. Within a few minutes, he was able to untangle the rest of the knot and handed the cord back to Ethan. "Thanks, man. Good thinking." He re-tied the two pieces back together and finished securing the cover. When Sam reappeared, conveniently after the tents had been constructed, he dumped a small armful of small twigs and branches next to the fire pit.

"Good job on that firewood, Sam," Aaron called from the entrance of his tent. "That should last us a whole twenty minutes!"

Sam was too busy to notice or care about Aaron's comment, dragging a giant Yeti cooler that his dad lent him for the weekend. He positioned it next to the fire pit and opened it up to reveal a bottle of whiskey and a case of beer with their food provisions.

"I was getting a bit thirsty!" he said with a smirk as he cracked open a can. "Anybody else?" The rest of the boys eagerly joined him, but Ethan hesitated.

"We're not supposed to have any booze in the park..." he began. "We're all underage; what if somebody reports us?"

"Relax," Sam said dismissively, pushing back his dark hair. "We haven't seen anybody for hours!" Watching his friends slurp down their beers, Ethan shrugged and took one. "Just make sure we pick up all the trash," he added before taking his first sip.

They gathered more wood after their beers and soon had a nice fire going. The twins took the two fishing poles and disappeared down the footpath to scout out good fishing spots. Sam, who had three beers in the time it took the rest of them to finish their first, decided it was time for a nap and retreated into the larger tent. Ethan and Jacob sat staring into the fire, enjoying the peace.

As much as Ethan enjoyed being deep in the woods, he also found himself uneasy as he took in their surroundings. He looked around and thought about how easy it would be for an animal, or person, to watch them from a distance without ever being detected. The forest floor was covered with a thick layer of soft pine needles that absorbed the sounds of footsteps.

That night they had hotdogs for dinner, as the twins returned empty-handed from their first fishing excursion. They did, however, find a baby deer and its dead mother down near the lake. They said it looked as if the deer had been shot, despite hunting season not starting for a few months. This brought the mood down significantly and the boys fell silent, picturing the baby deer curled up against its dead mother, as the twins described. Aaron said they had tried to catch it, but it always ran off to hide in the nearby brush, unwilling to leave its mother.

Sam made a joke that they were actually standing on an ancient Indian burial ground. They all laughed too easily, relieved to have any excuse to switch subjects. Soon they were passing the bottle of whiskey around and toasting to "old friends and new beginnings." As the surrounding woods got darker, Ethan couldn't help but think about how remote their campsite was and how exposed he felt sitting there with his back to the shadows of the tree line. He thought about the dead deer. He did his best to shake the feeling and enjoy his time with his buddies. The whiskey helped a bit.

The next morning, he and Jacob took the poles and tried their luck. They managed a few decent sized trout by the time their stomachs growled for lunch, and they took their spoils to share with the others. Ethan kept his eyes peeled for the dead deer or its baby, but saw no signs of them.

Sam wasn't all too interested in fishing, although he had no hesitation to help himself to the trout. He spent the rest of the day exploring the woods with the twins in hopes of finding a larger supply of firewood since they had burned through their supply already. As the sun dipped below the tops of the trees, he emerged from the footpath.

"Jacob, Ethan! Come check out this place that we found!" Sam cried. Jacob and Ethan obliged, stretching as they rose from their stump seats. He led them down the footpath towards the lake, but then veered off the path as they neared the water. "It's not far from here," he assured them. After struggling through the overgrown foliage for another twenty minutes, they finally surfaced and saw Aaron and Tommy smiling and waving to them from atop a large boulder. It jutted out from the side of the mountain, making a platform that overlooked the valley and lake. Getting to the top was tough but exciting, and the view once they made it was worth the sweat and scratches. Graffiti was scrawled over the rock wall that connected to the back of the boulder, and the surface was littered with cigarette butts and bits of trash.

"Isn't it great?" Sam exclaimed. He stood near the front edge of the boulder and held his arms out to his sides. "I feel like Simba on fucking Pride Rock!"

"It's a perfect smoke spot," Jacob admitted, already pulling out a small bag of pre-rolled joints from his pocket. They lit two joints and passed them back and forth between the five of them. This was how Ethan pictured the camping trip. Not necessarily getting high, but all of them hanging out together having a good time. Sam stood and brushed off the seat of his jeans.

"I gotta take a piss," he grunted, before descending the side of the boulder and disappearing behind some trees. He was gone for a few minutes when Jacob spoke.

"He's probably taking a huge dump, he could've just pissed off of the rock, like this!" He stood and walked out to the front edge of the boulder and unzipped his pants. A pale-yellow stream arched down from Jacob's body, disappearing into the trees below. It was almost picturesque if it wasn't so vulgar. "You're welcome!" He called down to any plants and animals he might have just baptized, laughing as he zipped up.

"Hey, what's the plan for dinner?" Tommy spoke up. "I'm getting some serious munchies."

"Me too!" Aaron chimed in, chuckling to himself as if he just told a hilarious joke.

"What about Sam?" Ethan asked.

Jacob shrugged. "I'm sure we'll run into him on the way back to camp." As dusk set in, the boys made their way back down the side of the boulder one by one.

Along the way back to camp, each boy gathered as many sticks as they could carry so they could cook up more hot dogs. It was already dark by the time they reached their site, so Jacob and the twins got to work starting a fire. Sam was there waiting for them. He told them he got thirsty and figured the rest of them would just come back to camp shortly after anyway. He chugged the rest of the beer he was holding and belched loudly before grabbing a second. *He'll fit right in at college,* Ethan thought to himself. Sam was the largest of them all and already demonstrated the typical frat boy qualities.

They ate dinner in relative silence, too busy stuffing their mouths with reheated BBQ chicken that Aaron and Tommy's mother had packed for them. She also packed potatoes wrapped in tin foil that they tossed into the hot embers to roast. Ethan decided he could never sustain himself on the hunter-gatherer diet he once imagined during those camping trips with his father. You just can't beat barbeque chicken. He went into his tent to change into warmer clothing and immediately noticed his gun case was out and opened. The gun was nowhere to be seen.

"Who's been through my stuff?" Ethan said angrily as he re-emerged from the tent flap. The other boys had moved on from dinner and were now roasting marshmallows. He was met with looks of confusion. "My gun is missing." he said when no one responded.

"You brought a *gun* with you?" Sam asked, raising an eyebrow.

"No one's touched your stuff, Ethan. Are you sure you didn't misplace it?" Jacob suggested.

"I haven't touched it since we set up camp yesterday and now the case is wide open and the gun is gone!" Ethan explained, sounding more panicked than he would like. He was looking at Sam, who now seemed preoccupied with poking the fire with a stick.

"Why did you bring a gun?" Aaron asked.

"Probably afraid of bears," Tommy quipped. The twins laughed together and high-fived.

"Sam, did you touch the gun?" Ethan asked pointedly. He was the only one who had the time to do it.

"What? No!" Sam said back with matched intensity. "I didn't even know you had one with you."

"You saw it in the parking area, you asked me about it," Ethan said.

"Dude, I just thought it was a weird tackle box or something. I swear I didn't touch your gun." Sam held his free hand up in a mock "scouts honor" motion.

"Where is it, then?" Ethan's heart was pounding in his chest. His dad would murder him if he lost his gun. "It's not in my tent anywhere."

"We'll look for it in the morning when it's light out; it's probably just covered with some clothing." Jacob tried to reassure him. "Come on, have a marshmallow. Grab a beer. We'll find it tomorrow when we pack everything back up."

Ethan wasn't entirely comfortable with the whereabouts of the gun being unknown, but he took a marshmallow anyway and speared it on the end of a stick to roast over the fire. He couldn't stop watching Sam, who seemed to avoid his gaze. After a long, uncomfortable silence, Tommy spoke.

"We should tell a ghost story or something. All part of the camping experience." He was trying to alleviate the tension.

"I've got one," Sam said, staring into the flames. "It's about a bunch of friends from high school. It was the summer before they all left for college. They all got accepted into different schools, far away from each other." He looked around at his friends. "All of them... except one." Sam looked directly at Ethan when he said this. "This one guy soon grew jealous of his friends. So jealous, in fact, that he decided he didn't want them to leave him behind. He planned a trip for them to all go out deep into the woods."

"Oh, fuck you, Sam," Ethan swore.

"Come on Sam, knock it off." Jacob started, but Sam continued over him. He pulled out a cigarette and lit it.

"This *friend* brought a gun with him, with exactly five bullets," he said, with smoke trailing from his mouth. "He knew what he had to do so that they could never leave him. One night, when they were all asleep, he took his gun and pointed it directly at his sleeping friend's face. BAM!" Sam yelled. "The other friends heard the first shot and came rushing out of their tent to see what happened. He picked them off as they approached his tent. BAM! BAM! BAM!" He paused, for added effect. "Then, with his last bullet, he points the gun at his own head and..." Somewhere in the woods a branch snapped, and Sam fell silent. The boys listened for more sounds, but none came.

"Okay then," Aaron said quietly. He took a swig of whiskey and passed it to Tommy, who did the same. He offered the bottle to Ethan, who shook his head. Sam reached past him to take the bottle. At that moment, a man's voice boomed out from the darkness.

"Put that bottle down, son."

The bottle slipped from Sam's hand and shattered at Ethan's boots. The boys jumped to their feet, trying to hide their empty beer cans from view.

"Y'all sit down now!" The man said aggressively. Ethan's blood turned to ice when he heard a shotgun being cocked. A man appeared at the edge of the clearing. As he came closer to the fire,

Ethan could see the man was holding the shotgun and was followed by two other men. They all dressed the same, wearing dark green coveralls with boots and wide-brimmed hats. They also had thick utility belts with flashlights, ropes, and a knife. Ethan guessed they were park rangers. The one holding the shotgun was taller than the other two and reminded Ethan of one of the football coaches from his high school.

"What do we have here?" The man spoke again. "You boys know that alcohol isn't permitted here on park grounds."

"Sorry, sir, we didn't know!" Tommy blurted out, rising from his seat. The man swung around and pointed the shotgun at Tommy's chest. "I said sit down!" He hollered. Tommy sat, quieted.

"I think these boys knew," the second man said. His scraggly red beard clung to his face in patches. "I'd say they're nothing but a bunch of little liars!" The third man let out a harsh laugh, then spat dark tobacco juice on the ground. The first man kept his gun aimed at Tommy's chest.

"Now I want all of you to put your hands behind your head and stand up. Slowly." The man said. Ethan and his friends glanced around at each other before following the man's orders. "Turn around." The boys slowly turned their backs to the men, uncertain of what would happen next. Ethan made eye contact with Jacob. His forehead was slick with sweat.

"Eyes forward!" barked the second man, whose voice sounded much closer than before. Ethan heard Jacob grunt in surprise as the man's hands roughly patted him down. When he pulled out the baggie of pre-rolled joints, he cried out delight. "Ah-a! What do we have here?" He stuffed the bag into his pocket and made his way over to Ethan. Ethan was starting to understand these men were not rangers, and that realization put a knot in his gut. The smell of alcohol came off the man in waves as he groped Ethan's body.

Under the watchful eye of the man with the shotgun, the third man had started the pat-down procedure at the other end of the line. Aaron was saying something that Ethan couldn't make out, but it resulted in a slap to the back of his head. Aaron stood quietly after that. On Tommy, they quickly discovered his small pocketknife and confiscated it, making Ethan think about the missing gun.

"All clear, boss." The second man spoke as he finished frisking Sam. He toed the broken bottle of whiskey at Sam's feet. "What a pity," he mumbled.

"Next order of business," the boss announced, walking around to face the boys. "We are going to find out who *this* belongs to." He reached behind his back and pulled out a 9mm handgun. Ethan's father's gun. Sam's head immediately whipped around to face Ethan, who could only open his mouth, speechless. The boss laughed. "I guess that was pretty easy then. Is this your gun, boy?" He held the gun out for Ethan to see. Nervously, Ethan nodded. These men must have been through their campsite while they were out on the rock. He was even more shocked when the man slapped the gun into his hand. "Come with me."

The boss placed a meaty hand on the back of Ethan's neck and steered him so he was standing a few feet from the rest of his friends. One man shoved Sam to fill the gap that Ethan left in the lineup.

"These two," the boss said, walking around the twins. "Pick one." Ethan looked at the man blankly. Then at Aaron and Tommy.

"I—I don't know—," Ethan started.

"I SAID PICK ONE!" the man roared, making them all jump.

"Tommy!" Ethan blurted out, not knowing what he had just done.

"And which one of you might be Tommy?" The boss was standing behind them now, his head jutting between theirs. The sudden transition in the man's voice as it went from fury to soothing calm was unsettling.

Tommy shakily raised his hand up from behind his head. "Nice to meet you, Tommy." The man said coldly. He stepped back and raised his shotgun and aimed at the back of Tommy's head. Ethan and the other boys screamed as they watched Tommy's head explode into a shower of blood and brain matter. Ethan would never forget the sound or sight. Aaron fell to the ground with his brother, screaming wildly. He made a move to tackle the boss, but was met with a swift kick to the face. He slumped next to his dead brother, subdued. Jacob moved to come to his aid but stopped when the smaller, boozy-smelling man pulled a large hunting knife out and poked, almost delicately, at his chest with it. Sam made no move, just stared in silent horror at what remained of Tommy's head.

Mark held out his hand to silence his wife, Julie, but she had stopped talking to listen to the sound of pained screams coming through the trees. They sent chills down her spine. The two sat for a moment, bristling with alarm as the screaming came to an abrupt end.

"That was a gunshot, wasn't it? Do you think they're hurt?" she asked him anxiously, getting to her feet.

"I don't know," he answered.

"Fireworks?" she suggested hopefully. "Maybe it was one of those mortar things..." He shook his head.

"No, those have two booms, one to launch and one when it explodes." They listened for anything else that could imply fireworks, but the woods around them were now eerily silent. Mark spoke first. "We better head over to see if everyone is okay." He went to the tent and returned with a pair of flashlights.

"Mark, wait. If it was a gunshot, shouldn't we go to the park office to get help?" Julie said. He paused and thought about it.

"Maybe... I really don't know. It sounded like someone was hurt badly, but you're right. It could be dangerous." He ran his fingers through his hair, frustrated. "You go back to the office and call the police. I have to go see if they need help. Immediate help." Julie grabbed his arm.

"No, Mark. We are not splitting up in the woods, at night, after hearing a possible gunshot. You're not at work right now, you do *not* have to rush off to save someone."

"But—" he protested.

"No!" She cut him off. "It's at least a twenty-minute hike back to the office. Who knows how far away those people are?" Mark knew she was right. The way those screams echoed through the woods made it clear they were coming from quite a distance.

"We need to hurry, then." Mark finally answered. The two took off at a run.

Ethan's hands were sweating as he raised his gun and pointed it at the boss. Tears threatened to blind him until they streamed down the sides of his face.

"Do it, Ethan!" Jacob yelled. "Kill these motherfuckers!" The other two men were crouching behind Sam and Jacob, using their bodies as shields. The boss laughed.

"Go ahead, son. Get a taste." He held his arms out to the side, shotgun dangling loosely from his right hand. Ethan took aim at him. His hand was shaking so badly he had to steady it with his other hand. He braced himself and pulled the trigger. *Click.*

"You've got a pair after all." the boss mused. "Do you really think I'd be stupid enough to hand you back your gun without taking all the bullets first?" Ethan struggled to release the clip. He knew how to shoot a gun, but he was less familiar with the moving parts. When he found the release button, the clip slid out; empty.

The third man came and took the gun out of Ethan's hand. With a zip tie, he secured Ethan's wrists together behind his back. The second man tied Aaron, who sat there numbly staring at his brother. "Stand up," he ordered gruffly, prodding Aaron in the back with his boot.

"James," the boss spoke, "take those two over that way." He gestured towards the trees vaguely with the shotgun. "David, take this one." He nodded at Aaron.

The man named James shoved Sam and Jacob hard and marched them into the dark woods, poking at their backs occasionally with his knife. David spat again and took Aaron by the arm and led him off in a different direction. Ethan was soon left alone with the boss. He couldn't bring himself to look at Tommy without a wave of nausea twisting his gut.

"You, come with me." The boss approached Ethan and pushed him down the footpath toward the lake. As they got farther away from their campsite, the light from the fire faded. Somewhere nearby, he could hear one of the men, James, telling Sam and Jacob to sit down and hold still. The boss put a hand on Ethan's shoulder, bringing him to a halt when they heard the sounds of a struggle. A man cried out in pain. Someone was crashing through the woods clumsily.

"Run, Jacob! Get help!" Sam's voice cried out. They listened as Jacob fell to the ground, grunting loudly. Then he screamed. Ethan cringed when he heard the repeated sound that a knife makes when it cuts into a slab of meat. Jacob's screams became distorted. His voice sounded strangled, and his cries gurgled before he went quiet. Ethan bent over and retched as he pictured what was happening to his best friend.

"Everything under control, James?" the boss called out.

"Motherfucker bit me!" James answered angrily. The boss chuckled softly and squatted down next to Ethan.

"Why are you doing this to us?" Ethan said after spitting out the residual bile in his mouth. The boss grabbed him by his shirt and dragged him to the nearest tree. Ethan kicked at him as hard as he could. His left foot contacted the man's knee, causing him to go down. With his arms still tied behind his back, Ethan struggled to his feet. He kicked at the man's head, but the boss caught his leg as he came in for the second kick and stood abruptly, holding Ethan's leg tight to his torso. This caused Ethan to lose his balance and land hard on his back.

Searing pain ripped through his right arm as Ethan landed and he heard a loud snap. He cried out but was silenced when the boss put all his weight on his knee straight into Ethan's gut. He punched Ethan in the face, hard. The force of the impact between that man's fist and the hard-packed earth made his head spin. He hit him again. Two, three times until Ethan was barely conscious. Blood spattered his nose and mouth and he blinked, disoriented. The boss slung his limp body against the base of a nearby tree and tied him to it with a thick rope he pulled off his utility belt. The last thing Ethan saw was the man walking away into the darkness.

When Mark and Julie finally pulled into the office parking lot, it was empty. They ran up the two steps and tried the office door, but of course, it was locked. Julie pounded on the door regardless.

"Office hours are six am to ten pm." Mark said despairingly. He looked at his watch and saw it was well past midnight. They each tried their cell phones in vain. Mark banged the door frame a few more times. Around the side of the office, Julie found an old payphone. It looked ancient, probably hadn't been used in years. But she picked the phone up and dialed 911.

"Hello? Yes, I'd like to report a..." she trailed off, trying to describe the situation. "We're at the Blue Ridge Lake reservation. We think we heard a gunshot and some screaming. Can you please send someone out here to check it out?" She paused as she listened. "I see. Please tell them to hurry!" She hung up. Mark appeared at the edge of the office's front porch. "Did you get the police?"

She nodded. "The dispatcher said it might take up to two hours for someone to get out here. She told us to wait here at the office." They walked around to the front steps and sat. After a moment, Mark spoke.

"We're really just going to sit here and wait for them? People might need immediate help..." he trailed off as they heard footsteps approaching from within the office. A light went on and Henry, the old man who had checked them in appeared at the door.

"What's going on?" he asked as he stepped out onto the porch, pulling on a worn denim jacket. Mark and Julie told him what they had heard. He thought for a minute, his bushy eyebrows furrowing. "I think I might have an idea of who it is. We've been having some issues with poaching on the reservation the past few years." Henry disappeared back into the office briefly before reemerging holding an old revolver pistol and a .38 special. "Do you know how to handle a gun?" He was speaking to Mark.

"Me? Uh, no. Not really." Mark chuckled nervously. "I'm an emergency responder, I usually just patch the holes those things make."

"I can shoot." Julie spoke up. Henry turned and looked at her with surprise, then nodded. He handed her the .38 and said, "We'll take my truck, it's around back."

"What about the police?" Mark asked. "They told us to wait here for them." The old man shook his head.

"I'm willing to bet they'll take their sweet time getting here. Unless somebody finds and reports an actual body, they just assume it's likely to be a waste of their time driving all the way out into the mountains. It usually is. Kid goes missing, parents panic and call the cops. Nine times outta ten, the kid shows up before they even get here. This park, unfortunately, has a history of "crying wolf" to them, so to speak."

When Ethan woke up, the first thing he felt was his right arm, throbbing. How long had he been unconscious? In the distance, he could see that their fire had long gone out. It was just barely getting light. His body was stiff and numb and the chill in the air made it worse. He pulled against the rope, but it was tied tight, and the pain in his arm forced him to stop. Panting from his effort and sheer panic, Ethan did the only thing he could do.

"Help! Somebody! Help! Please, somebody help me!" He screamed. Ethan heard footsteps crunching toward him and screamed louder, but his heart sank to his stomach when he saw the three men who appeared before him.

"Finally awake, I see." The boss sneered at him, his shotgun was missing. "Your other friends kept us company while you were out." David and James both chuckled at this, and Ethan noticed with horror they all had dark bloodstains on their clothing. "Untie him and let him see our handiwork." James cut through the rope with his knife, which had dried blood on the blade, while David held onto Ethan.

They yanked him to his feet, cut the zip tie holding his hands, and shoved him in the direction they wanted him to go. He thought about running, but his body was still so stiff and sore from being tied down to that tree he knew he wouldn't make it far. He cradled his injured arm to his chest, his mind racing through all the possibilities and outcomes. None looked good for him.

Ahead of him, he could see a form on the ground. He knew it was Jacob before he got close enough to see. Jacob was lying on his back in the dirt with his hands still tied behind him. His skin had turned a pale, waxy yellow and his face was twisted into a horrific sneer. His chest and stomach were covered in stab wounds, some gouging deep enough to spill some of his intestines out the side. His eyes seemed to follow Ethan and the men as they pushed him further along.

The path opened up to a small clearing, and Ethan wished he hadn't looked. He saw Sam, sprawled on his stomach in the dirt and pine needles with his legs pulled apart. His pants were missing, and the dried blood made it evident what had happened to him. He still had a rope twisted around his neck, used as both murder weapon and harness. His eyes bulged, and it looked like he had bitten halfway through his tongue during the struggle. Empty beer cans from the boys' cooler were scattered around the clearing, making Ethan wonder how long Sam and Aaron were tortured like this. He looked away before he got sick again, his empty stomach threatening to upheave again. He could see the lake through the trees, the surface of the water was sparkling as the sky grew lighter.

"Put up a good fight, that one," James said, his voice filled with sickening glee.

"Sure did," agreed David. "Reminded me of that dog we got when we were teenagers back in Jackson. You remember that?" James laughed. "Arrooo! Arroo!" He howled and David laughed, making Ethan sick to his stomach. He turned away from the sight, only to see Aaron staring up at him with glassy eyes. He was slumped over the trunk of a tree that had fallen. His face was barely recognizable, he was beaten so badly. Several of his teeth littered the forest floor before him. Then Ethan saw the shotgun resting against the trunk behind him.

David took Ethan's arm and led him around to the other side of the tree. A hole had been torn through Aaron's back, nearly cutting him in half, and with sick horror, Ethan came to realize that the shot had come from the inside. Aaron's pants had also been removed, and the tip of the shotgun was caked with blood and excrement.

"This one here called us fags while we were taking care of his buddy," David said. "I told him to shut up, but he kept going. The way that shotgun slid in sure made it seem like it wasn't the first time he had something stuck up his pretty little ass." This got more hoots of laughter from James. Ethan looked at the boss, who looked over the scene with grim seriousness.

"Let's get this finished up, it's getting late," he said in a tone that sent chills through Ethan. *They've done this before.* In the growing light, Ethan could see now that he must be James and David's father. The two men were still guffawing and carrying on when the boss whistled sharply. They fell silent. In the distance, they could hear a diesel engine crunching through the overgrown trail. They could see nothing, but they heard a car door slam.

"Hello?" A woman's voice called out, followed by a man's. Someone was looking for them. David walked back to the trunk to stand by his father, leaving James, the smaller man by Ethan's side. All of them were distracted by whoever was searching through the woods.

Ethan's heart raced. This could be his only chance. Adrenaline coursed through his body, giving him a newfound energy. Without thinking, he lurched forward and buried his shoulder into James' side. Grabbing the shotgun off the trunk, he took off through the trees. He heard James swear, but he didn't turn to see if he was being chased. He was headed toward the water. It was the opposite direction of the people in the truck, but he couldn't risk trying to get past the other two men.

He crashed through the woods, small branches slapping at his face and legs as he ran. At the water's edge, he didn't hesitate and plunged straight in. The water was freezing, it took his breath right out of him. He could hear the men in pursuit close behind him. He let the shotgun sink, as he now needed his good arm to do most of the work that the other couldn't. The cold water made it difficult for him to move, but he swam at least twenty yards before he turned around to see if they were following him into the water. The three men stood at the shoreline. The boss loaded a new clip into Ethan's father's gun. He aimed at Ethan's head, bobbing above the water. Ethan ducked down below the water and tried to put more distance between them, but he couldn't stay under for long. He resurfaced, gasping for air that the icy water seemed to suck out of him.

The boss took aim once more and fired. Ethan flinched as he heard the shot ring out, but the water around him remained undisturbed. The boss took another shot. Nothing. Ethan watched as he removed the clip from the gun angrily. "Blanks!" The boss swore. Ethan remembered his father on their camping trips.

"Bears and other animals will run away if they hear the gunshot, you don't need to actually shoot them. It's safer that way if you're going to have a loaded gun lying around with little boys like you." His father explained to him once. It felt like forever ago.

"But," he added. "Just in case, I always leave a few live rounds at the bottom of the clip, in case the blanks don't do the trick."

Ethan's relief soon vanished as he watched the boss empty the clip into his hand. He found the real bullets at the bottom. Ethan was struggling to keep his head above the water; his entire body was numb. He closed his eyes as the boss took aim once more. BAM! There was no mistake in the difference in sound, but he missed. The bullet hitting the water only a foot away from his head. The boss took a knee to steady his aim, and Ethan could practically feel the gun lining up directly with him. *This is it,* he thought, closing his eyes once more as his limbs gave out. If he doesn't get me, I will drown anyway. BAM!

Ethan opened his eyes in shock to see the boss slumped forward, face-down in the shallow water. James and David had their backs to him, arms raised. He could see someone coming down the path to the lake, a woman with blonde hair. She was holding a small pistol. The old man from the park office followed close behind her, gun drawn. He looked ten years younger than when he had checked them in. A third man came with them. He saw Ethan's head, barely staying afloat, and ran past David and James, who were now on their knees. Ethan tried to swim back to the shore, but the cold was shutting his body down, sapping all of his remaining energy. He dipped under. He barely noticed when the man reached him and hauled him back to dry land.

Mark dragged the limp body of the boy out of the water and pumped his chest a few times. He could see that his arm was broken, but otherwise, he seemed relatively unharmed compared to the others he saw in the woods. He pumped the boy's chest again and was prepared to perform CPR when the boy heaved and spat out a mouthful of water. "Good boy, good boy, get it all out," Mark said encouragingly, turning him to his side. Behind him, Julie kept her gun aimed at the two men while Henry tied their hands behind them with the ropes they had found. The boy stopped coughing up water but sobbed, curled on his side. "It's going to be okay, you're safe now." He spoke softly, rubbing the boy's back. "Let's get you out of those clothes and dried off."

When they returned to the park office, they found two state troopers milling about near their patrol car. Once they spoke with Henry, they immediately radioed for an ambulance and backup. The parking lot was soon filled with flashing lights and local police. David and James were arrested and taken away. A detective came and spoke with Ethan to get his statement as a paramedic splinted his arm. Mark and Julie stood by his side, listening in horror. As he finished telling the story, his parents pulled into the parking lot, along with Jacob's parents. Sam's father showed up behind them with Aaron and Tommy's parents in his truck. His mother burst into tears the second she saw him and ran to hug him.

"Ethan! Are you okay? What happened, where are the others?" Her voice was tight with concern. He started to retell what had happened, but broke down when he saw the other parents realize that their sons were not there. "Shh, honey. It's okay." She held him to her chest, rocking him gently. They watched together, as the medics pushed carts carrying his friends in zipped body bags. Ethan would never forget the sound of the twins' mother shrieking when she pushed past them, insisting on seeing her sons. Their father had to catch her and turn her away, her screams echoing through the park. Jacob's parents sat together quietly, mourning their only son. Sam's father was talking to some officers, his voice rising in anger, unable to accept what they were telling him.

"Dad," Ethan spoke finally. "Those blank bullets in the gun, they saved my life." His father looked at him, confused. "He tried to shoot me when I was in the water." Ethan's father said nothing, but hugged him and his mother with tears in his eyes. Ethan and his parents also hugged and thanked Julie, Mark, and Henry for their heroism. Then they rode in silence to the hospital, where Ethan's arm was put in a cast. The detective who took his statement at the park office approached them.

"Those two men are going to be locked away for good, with their records. It's over now. We found their camp not far from where you and your friends were staying. Their father was a wanted man in a few nearby states; it looks like they were hiding out there for quite some time."

He spoke softly, carefully choosing his words. Ethan said nothing and looked away, thinking of his friends. The detective put a hand on his shoulder. "It will take time, but you survived this. You will get through this." He offered several pamphlets to Ethan's parents about PTSD therapy and treatment. Ethan just wanted to shut the world out. He wanted to go home and curl up under the blankets on his bed and stay there for eternity. He survived, but he doubted he would ever live again.

1999

I T WAS THE SUMMER of 1999. I was spending my afternoon down by the creek behind the Heinsohn farm, throwing stones into the water. My friend Matt moved away at the end of the school year; otherwise, he'd have been with me. Probably doing something more exciting than just throwing stones. Although he only moved an hour or so away, it might as well be across the country when I relied on my parents to drive me everywhere. I was turning twelve next month and hoped that he could come out for my birthday, or possibly even sleep over.

I was lost in my thoughts, watching the stones disappear through the water's murky surface, when I heard a boy's voice.

"Hey! You're gonna scare all the fish away!" I turned to see a boy I didn't recognize standing a few yards away from me, holding a makeshift fishing pole. He had fashioned it out of a long tree branch with a string tied to the end.

"There's no fish in here. Nothing worth catching, anyway," I replied, trying to appear knowledgeable about the subject. The boy shrugged casually, his hand-me-down shirt and faded jean shorts hanging loosely on his body.

"Fishing's more for contemplating. That's what my dad says, anyway," he replied. "Do you want to hunt some crawdads with me?"

"Crawdads?" I repeated.

"Those little lobster guys that live in creeks like this. I bet there's a ton of them here."

"Oh—I call them 'crayfish,'" I said.

"Same thing. Some people call them prawns or river shrimp. It's just words. Whatever you call them, they're still fun to catch." I liked him instantly. His name was Zachary, but he preferred "Zach."

We spent a few hours picking up rocks and watching the crayfish skitter about in the shallow water. He was skilled at catching them without getting pinched. I was admittedly rusty with that part. He told me he and his parents moved into the old house a few miles down the road from where I lived. His father was working on fixing the house up, as nobody had lived there for some time.

After we scared all the crayfish away, I invited him to come back to my house for dinner. He thanked me but declined. He had to get home to help his mother. I found it a little odd because in my twelve years I had rarely given any thought to helping my mother with anything more than killing the occasional spider that found its way into the house. We decided to meet at the creek again the next day.

"Well, I think that's very sweet of him," my mother, Susan, stated that evening at the dinner table. I'd just finished telling her and my father about my new friend. "I wouldn't mind if you helped me with the dishes tonight, Adam." I rolled my eyes and groaned, but my dad gave me a look that said: "wash *and* dry."

"Where did you say they lived again?" My dad spoke after a bite of his mashed potatoes.

"Zach said they moved into the old house up on Walker Street." I shrugged.

"I thought that place was in pretty sad shape. I can't imagine anyone living there without a lot of work being done first," my dad continued, shoveling another helping of mashed potatoes into his mouth.

"His dad is rebuilding it," I said, growing defensive. I didn't care about the house Zach lived in, but my dad wouldn't let it go.

"We should take a quick drive up there after dinner to check it out. Maybe he could use some extra hands," he went on.

"Paul, leave them alone. You don't have to go sticking your nose in everybody's business," Susan scolded lightly. He shrugged in response and washed his mashed potatoes down with a swig of Sam Adams.

I was just about finished with the dishes when my dad clapped his hand on my shoulder, startling me.

"Come on, let's go check it out. You can introduce me to your new buddy."

We got into my dad's old Chevy and rumbled down the road. When I saw the house, my heart sank a little. It had been some time since I saw it last; I didn't realize how bad it had gotten. The house seemed to have collapsed into itself. The front door hung crookedly from one hinge, and most of the windows were broken. There were no cars or construction equipment in the driveway or yard.

"Huh," Dad grunted. He pulled into the driveway to turn around. "It doesn't look like anyone's been here for a while, kiddo. Are you sure this was the house he was talking about?" I didn't know what to say. I don't know why my dad cared so much. As we pulled out of the driveway, I thought I saw movement through one of the broken windows. Then again, it was probably a raccoon or something.

The next day it rained so hard that I could barely see the trees lining our property. I thought about my plans to meet with Zach at the creek. I would be drenched before I got ten feet from my house. I stared out the window for a long time, contemplating if I should still go, in case Zach was out there waiting for me. I grabbed my raincoat and boots out of the hall closet.

"Where do you think you're going?" My mom's voice came from behind me as I slipped into the boots. I turned around.

"I was supposed to meet with Zach today by the creek," I said simply. My mom pursed her lips.

"I don't think that's a great idea, honey. He's probably staying home today. Staying *dry*. You can hang out with him another day." I protested, but she held firm. I was not going outside after all. I paced the house tirelessly, hoping for the rain to let up.

It was still drizzling the following day, but not enough to keep me cooped up. The air outside was humid but smelled clean and pure. I trudged across the soggy lawn wondering if Zach would be at the creek that day. The creek was flooded, with debris collected along the banks. I looked around for Zach, but he wasn't there. I turned back to head home when I heard the splash-bloop of a large rock hitting the water. I wheeled around to see Zach standing on the opposite bank. He grinned at me and waved for me to follow him down the stream. I kept pace with him on my side of the creek and he took me to a section where some logs and branches had formed a dam.

"You can cross over here!" Zach called above the noise of the rushing water. It was much deeper here than upstream. The current made dark swells on either side of the makeshift bridge. Zach saw me eyeballing the water. "Come on, don't be a pussy! You can do it—I did it, no problem!" He beckoned with his arms. I had heard that word a few times, but each time it still struck me a little.

I took a tentative step onto the closest log. It wiggled a little but seemed sturdy enough otherwise. I looked up at Zach, whose eyes were fixed on me. Another step, reaching out to balance myself on a branch that protruded upwards. I kept moving forward until I reached midway and realized none of the branches ahead of me looked strong enough to support my weight.

"You have to crawl. Spread your weight out more," Zach encouraged me. I continued, not wanting to seem like a chicken. The first step I took made the branch sag a few inches into the water. I held on to whatever sticks and twigs I could to stay upright as the water pulled at my submerged foot. As I lifted my right foot to continue, the branch snapped, and my left foot plunged into the water up to my thigh. I grabbed for the smaller branches, but they didn't help. I kicked out, trying to find a rock or the bottom of the stream to no avail. I was falling backwards into the water, and I was pulling the branches down on top of me. The water was cold from the rain, catching my breath in my chest as I went under. The current swept me further as I struggled to get back to the surface.

Finally, I was able to get my head above water and I saw Zach watching me with a strange look on his face.

"Help me!" I cried out, still being dragged down by the current. This seemed to snap Zach out of that trance-like state he was in. He ran down the side of the stream until he was past me and plunged in. He swam out to me as I came by and grabbed my arm. The two of us eventually made it back to the bank, gasping for air. I was shaking badly, either from the cold water or adrenaline, or both. I looked over at Zach, expecting the same, but he seemed unphased by the cold.

"That was exciting," he said, eyes gleaming. I stared at him in disbelief.

"Are you kidding me? My mom is going to kill me!" I spat. "I could've drowned, no thanks to you."

"No thanks to me? I just saved your ass," Zach came back. "Only an idiot tries to swim against the current. I thought you would've known that, spending so much time here." I felt my cheeks burn and was thankful for the little heat that my anger provided me.

"I should never have listened to you," I said bitterly.

"If you hadn't, you would never know what it's like to *really* live." Zach's eyes were wild.

"You sound like a psycho. I don't have to almost drown to appreciate breathing." I snapped at him. Zach's face grew dark.

"Don't call me that." He looked different. He looked almost menacing with his chest heaving and dark hair matted down on his head.

"Whatever, man." I said, trying to deescalate the situation.

"But you did it!" He exclaimed brightly. "See? You're on the other side now." He waved his hands. I looked around. We were much farther downstream than I expected. I didn't want to even think about trying to cross the stream again. I would have to walk all the way down past the farm to where there was a small one-lane bridge for cars. From there it was at least an hour more to get home. I told Zach I had to get home to change out of my drenched clothes. He complained a little bit, but eventually, let me go in peace. I invited him to come with me, but he declined, saying he should go home to change clothes as well. I was partly relieved when he said no. I wasn't too eager to spend much more time with him that day, but I knew my mother would take it easier on me if I had a friend there.

During the long walk home, I kept feeling like someone was watching me. I saw Zach walk off in the opposite direction, but I couldn't help but get the idea out of my head that he was following me. Watching me.

Fortunately for me, my mother was out grocery shopping when I got home. The dry erase board had "Zucchini Lasagne tonight! Be home in a few hours..." scrawled on it in my mother's handwriting. I grimaced at the idea of zucchini replacing pasta.

As I changed my clothes, I heard a noise outside. I went to my window to investigate. It was Zach, standing in my backyard. He was still wearing the same clothes, but they looked dry somehow. He was holding something that looked like a dirty gray rag and beckoning for me to come outside. When I got to the door, something didn't feel right. Call it a gut feeling. I looked at that rag in his hand again and my stomach sank. It was a cat.

"Look what I found," he called out, holding it up. "It was stuck in some branches along the stream where we were. I made a face.

"Why would you bring it here?" I asked. Zach shrugged. "You followed me home with a dead cat?" I pushed.

"Well, yeah," he said, uncertain. "I thought it was cool. We can play 'Mad Scientist' and inspect it and stuff." He had me there. That did sound kind of cool. It wasn't too far off from when I used to do frog experiments with Matt by the stream. We would catch a frog and knock it on the head with a stick. Then we would time how long they would take to wake up and write it in our notebook. Some of the frogs never woke up, of course, but it was in the name of science. Besides, it's not like Zach *killed the cat*—it was already dead. We went to the shed where my father kept his tools.

An hour later, Zach disappeared into the woods, saying he had to get home to help his mother again. Coincidentally, my mom pulled into the driveway minutes after he disappeared into the woods. I helped my mom carry the grocery bags inside, thinking about the cat and what Zach had told me. My mom was talking about this new recipe she would try for dinner tomorrow night, and listening to her talking about mixing the ground beef with ground sausage made me nauseous.

I didn't eat much of her zucchini lasagna that night. After dinner, I went to bed early, much to the surprise of my parents.

"Are you feeling okay, sweetie?" My mom said, pressing the back of her hand against my forehead. I brushed her hand away and said I was just tired. This made her exchange a look with my dad, who said nothing. I lay in my bed that night, thinking about Zach and that cat.

At first, I was excited to "study" the drowned cat's body with him. We found a plank of scrap wood to secure it to—an "autopsy table," Zach called it. We used wire to stretch the arms and legs out, belly up. Then Zach came out of the shed with a hacksaw. "This is what vets use to tell if an animal has rabies," he said, holding the saw out for me to see. "We have to make sure it's safe before we do anything else." I wasn't sure if he was just making stuff up at this point for the game, or if he was serious.

I watched until he pressed the saw blade against the cat's neck. I looked away from the cat and focused on him. I heard everything as he set to work. His strokes were slow and deliberate.

"So, uh," I started. It took a few seconds to steady my voice. "My dad and I went to go see your house last night." Zach stopped and looked up at me. "And we didn't see any cars or construction stuff," I said tentatively. Zach shrugged and continued to saw at the cat's neck. I got a little queasy when I heard the saw hit wood.

"He packs everything up inside at night so nobody steals it. Do you have a plastic bag?" Zach's answer and complete change in direction caught me off guard. I nodded and ran to grab a bag from the kitchen. Through the kitchen window, I watched as Zach wiped the hacksaw off on a rag and put it back on the shelf. When I returned with the bag, he had an X-Acto knife in his hand.

Zach put the blade to the top of the cat's throat and made a long incision down the center. "My mom is trying to leave my dad," he said quietly as he worked, pulling the skin away from the flesh beneath. "She wants to take me with her." Another incision down the inside of the back leg. "This makes my dad real angry." He continues, cutting a ring around the bases of the hind feet.

I watch silently. Horrified, as he repeats this process with the front paws. Zach goes on. "They got into a big argument one night." He glanced at me for a moment, over the half-flayed cat. Zach's face was calm, but his eyes burned. "It doesn't help that he drinks so much." He returned his attention to the cat, pulling gently on the skin. "They think I'm asleep, but I'm listening from the stairs. I can hear him calling me names, saying I'm crazy. My mom knows I'm not. She defends me. I hear her cry out when he hits her. I grab my baseball bat," he continues. As I listened to what Zach was saying, I realized he was telling me about something that had already happened. It was like when people on TV get hypnotized and talk about memories like they're reliving it.

"I can hear them both screaming at each other as I creep down the stairs. He wants to take me to some doctor, but my mom says that *he's* the one who needs the doctor." Zach went on. "Her screams cut off right as I get to the kitchen doorway." He had untied the cat's hind legs and was pulling the skin off like a sweater. "This part is much easier when the body is still warm," he explained casually. As if he wasn't in the middle of telling me an extremely disturbing story. As if he had done this many, many times to animals that weren't already dead when he found them.

"What happened to your mother?" I asked, dreading his answer. Zach said nothing. He re-fastened the cat's hind legs to the board and made another long incision down the center of the belly.

"You have to be careful here. Too deep and you can cut open the stomach or guts and then you have a mess on your hands." I grimaced as he stuck his hand inside and pulled out the cat's organs. The smell was awful. I tried to keep from gagging as he pointed out the heart, the stomach, the bladder, the kidneys.

"Ah-ha!" Zach smiled at me and held something up. "The lungs." He gave them a gentle shake. He cut one open, and some foul-smelling water dribbled out. "Case closed. I can now confirm that the victim has indeed died of drowning, Officer," he said in a deep cartoonish voice. I thought I was going to be sick. "Let's get a body bag for this thing and put it to rest," he said, still ignoring my question.

We got a hefty bag and dumped the cat and its entrails into it, board and all. We wiped off the knife and put it back on my dad's workbench, got a shovel and set out into the woods. Neither of us spoke until after we piled a few rocks on top of the grave.

"Zach?" I started timidly. "What happened to your mom?" I repeated my question from earlier. He stared straight ahead and wiped his nose on his hand.

"I wasn't fast enough." He lifted his shirt slightly and I saw he had a deep gash in his side. I gasped. "Oh my god, dude. Is that from last night? How are you not—" and then part of me understood. Zach cocked his head and looked at the sky, which was getting dark.

"I gotta get home to help my mom. See you around." And with that, he left. He walked back into the woods, and I never saw him again. I didn't have to search around on the internet for long to discover the full story. I saw a picture of Zach and his parents. Double homicide followed by a suicide in that old house on Walker Street. It happened when I was in kindergarten.

To this day, the rational part of my brain tries to convince me that none of this ever happened. That I had probably seen that picture on the news when it happened. Then, in the summer of 1999, my brain made everything up out of boredom because my friend had moved away. It almost sounds plausible... but I know for a fact that if I go digging around in the woods behind my dad's shed, I will find those cat bones.

HOTEL

A WORD OF WARNING to my friends,
Don't mean to cause you strife
Listen close, I must speak softly
My advice might save your life

I travel for work,
and travel often.
A salesman by trade,
hard water to soften

Hotel rooms; a nomad's comfort
I journey far and wide
One fateful night in Saigon, I saw
Something by my side

I locked the door, forgot the latch
a careless man back then.
Somehow a creature got inside
I don't know how... or when

I blinked my eyes and sat up straight
Was my mind playing tricks?
But there it stood, right by my bed
holding up fingers; six.

"Six, what?" I thought, about to scream
I went for the light near the bed.
The light went on, but it was gone,
Could it have all been in my head?

That was many years ago
I try to forget that night
Safe in the states I continue my work
But I fear I'm still in its sight

I feel it watching as I sleep
Why won't it leave me alone
One more night, one more hotel
Tomorrow I go home

I lock my door, and now the latch
I've learned my lesson and more
One thing I failed to notice though,
Was the number on my door.

That night I woke with a sense of dread
I was alone, safe in my room
But something was watching from the door
The latch prevented my doom

The hallway was dark
Three inches of space
But through the cracked door
I could still see its face

It tried to get in to no avail
Long fingers on the frame
When the latch held strong, it began to wail
I heard it say my name

Always lock the doors, the latch
Regardless how safe you may feel
Something came for me that night
The boogeyman is real.

STOLEN LIFE

I

I WOKE UP WITH a start, my heart racing in my chest. Glancing outside, I checked the sky. It was still early. I had been having terrible visions in my sleep, but come morning, the images faded faster than stones tossed into the river. I pulled my legs out of my sleep sack and stood up slowly, stretching my arms above my head.

Stepping out into the misty morning air, I saw that Seng, my neighbor, was already outside. He had started working on building the bonfire, positioned in the village center. Seng worked quickly with his hands, chopping and sorting small branches into neat bundles with his *khet*. His dark hair fell in strands around his face and broad shoulders. Today was a big day for his family. His mate, Sho, had just birthed their second son a few nights ago.

Seng nodded at me as I approached. I crouched beside him quietly, joining him in breaking down the smaller pieces of kindling with my hands.

"It looks like the skies will be pleasant this day," I said cheerfully. Seng grunted in response. Seng didn't quite enjoy my company, or anybody else's for that matter. It was a wonder when Sho chose him to be her mate. We worked in relative silence as other clan members began to emerge from their hutches and join us. Once we had stacked the kindling bundles at the base of the firepit, we started to pile larger branches atop, until the pyre was towering above the tallest man's head, who happened to be Seng.

There was a small noise and Sho emerged from their hutch, carrying the infant. A smaller boy, barely 2 summers old, trailed behind her, clutching at her skirts. Most of the men kept their distance as the women of the clan gathered close to greet Sho and her boys, offering kind words and blessings. I saw my younger sister, Kuri, wrinkle her nose when Sho uncovered the baby's face from his blanket. She was still young, but would probably be ready to find a mate of her own in a few seasons.

The rest of the day was spent preparing for the naming ceremony of Seng and Sho's son. The younger men, including me, were sent out to collect fish that were trapped in our river nets and any smaller animals caught in snares. The children were sent out into the nearby trees to gather roots, berries, and nuts, though I suspected that a small portion of their findings were consumed on the spot. The women decorated the village center with flowers and brightly colored fabrics draped over the entrance to each hutch.

I made my way back to the village as the sun began to dip below the tallest trees, with seven fat silverfish and a small rabbit slung over my shoulder. Smaller fires surrounded the village. The central bonfire remained unlit, but I could smell a variety of soups and stews simmering over the smaller flames. I laid the fish down in a large basket with the other collected fish and took the rabbit to my mother in our family's hutch.

I found her making a paste by scraping ochre between a large flat stone and a smaller rock. Generations of use had worn a smooth groove in the center of the large stone, perfect for cradling the ingredients. My sister was using the paste to create a delicate design of traditional dots and lines along her cheekbones and brow.

"Tel, you should have been back sooner." My mother scolded lightly, not taking her eyes off her work. "It's not safe to be outside the village past dark."

I sighed. "It's not dark yet, plenty of time." I held the rabbit up for her to see. "I brought this for you." She looked at me then, pausing to brush a stray strand of hair out of her eyes. She eyed the rabbit for a moment.

"Bring it to Ulak. He needs it more than we do."

"Ulak doesn't need it. He's just acting that way so that the rest of the village keeps him fed." I said, offended that she would turn her nose up at my gift so quickly.

"They took his wife, Tel. They would have taken him too if the men didn't stop him from going after her. You know this." I did know this, and my face burned in shame. I was supposed to be standing watch that night, only one moon earlier.

At 14, all the boys must start taking turns tending the fires that surround the village at night. I was nearly 15 when it happened, but I had gotten distracted by my friend, Renai. She was coming of age when she was to choose a mate, so naturally, she was on my mind often.

Drums sounded outside. The ceremony was about to begin. I quickly made my way through the growing crowd to Ulak's hutch and presented him with the rabbit.

"Thank you for your kindness, Tel." The man said as he took it from me. At that moment, I felt guilty about what I had said to my mother just moments ago. He was an older man, not quite as old as the Elders, but he could never become one because he had used his *vaen*, or "second life" many seasons ago—when he was barely out of his youth, only a few summers older than I was then. He bowed his head again in thanks, and I returned the bow politely and retreated from his hutch.

Outside, villagers gathered around the now blazing fire, with Seng and his family standing before the six elders. Moashi, the eldest, raised her hands to silence the crowd. She began to speak as my mother and Kuri approached my side for the ceremony.

"It is a great honor and blessing to welcome this new child into our clan. Seng and Sho have given us another son, whose name shall be... Anok!" The crowd cheered, but I heard my mother gasp as she heard her mate's name announced. My father's name. Seng stood tall and unwavering, his face serious as Moashi took the infant's arm in her hand and made a delicate slice with her small obsidian blade. The child screamed, but Sho and Moashi held him still as another elder came forth with a small hollowed-out bone to collect the blood. As two other elders attended to Anok's cut with healing salves and cloth wrapping, Moashi sealed the bone in beeswax, preserving the blood. This would serve as Anok's *vaen*... should he ever need it.

"The blood is tied to the soul!" Moashi cried out, raising the newly sealed *vaen*. "A man who takes another's blood does not become stronger—he becomes *lost*." This, she said after every naming ceremony. She walked slowly toward the Elders' hutch, where each clan member's *vaen* were secured safely.

Soon, people began to sing, eat, and dance, celebrating the newest member of the clan. I searched for Renai among the dancing bodies silhouetted by firelight, but she was nowhere to be found. I could see Sho comforting her sons, both of whom were crying at this point. In the distance, I saw Seng following Moashi into the Elders' hutch, his usual scowl deepening as he glanced over his shoulder. I frowned. Only elders were allowed in that sacred space—what business did he have there? My thoughts were quickly interrupted when Kuri bumped hips with me.

"Are you just going to stand there or are you going to dance, brother?" She laughed, enjoying the festivities. I shoved her away playfully, laughing as well, and joined her, but throughout the night I continued to look for Renai with no luck. Perhaps she was avoiding me after our last encounter—the night that Ulak's wife was taken.

II

I woke up abruptly to the sounds of wailing and heavy footsteps outside our hutch. Before I could push through the deerskin entrance, Seng yanked it open and glared down at me.

"S-Seng!" I gasped. "What is it?" My mother and Kuri bolted upright in their sleep sacks at the sound of the disturbance. "The *vaen* of the elders have been stolen," Seng responded curtly, his eyes scanning our belongings. "We're searching every hutch. If they're not found, you will attend the search party."

Without permission to enter, Seng entered our home, tossing what little belongings we had to the side. My family and I were waiting outside when he emerged. "Gather your hunting gear, we head out soon to track the thief. They must've gone to the woods." And with that, Seng stomped off to the next hutch.

"Why would someone steal the *vaen* of the elders?" Kuri asked, her eyes wide with fear. My mother looked as though she was about to answer my sister's question, but instead turned to me. "Tel, you need to be careful when you join the hunting party today. Take your father's *khet* and bow." I gaped at her. I had only been allowed to partake in collecting fish and small prey from the snares until now. Mother nodded at me reassuringly and pointed back to our hutch with her eyes.

Inside, I opened the soft leather wrap that held my father's weapons. I grabbed the *khet* first. The wooden handle was worn smooth from use, but the blade was still sharp enough to skin a deer. It felt heavy in my hand. It had been seasons since the bow was last used, but the sinew was still strong and pliable. With the bow slung over my shoulder, I attached the leather bundle that held my father's arrows to my waist, next to my father's *khet*.

As I reemerged from the hutch, I saw my mother look at me with a mixture of pride and sadness. I had been just a young boy when my father died, and Kuri... only an infant. We touched foreheads quickly and I bounded off to where three other men in Seng's tracking group were gathering. As we headed into the woods, I caught a glimpse of Renai looking at me from one of the nearby hutches. The sight of her made my blood run hot, filling me with strength and courage.

III

The hunting group made its way quickly through the nearby forest, where the ground had been trampled smooth by the women and children who collected herbs, fruits, and nuts daily. As we went deeper into the trees, the pathways became more deliberate and narrow, used by the hunters and young men who tended to the fishing nets and snares. I spotted a fox caught in the snare I'd retrieved the rabbit from the day before and instinctively moved toward it, but Maro, one of the men, stopped me.

"When we return," he said. I nodded and continued with the group. As Naav, the best tracker in the village, took the lead, I couldn't help but wonder who would steal the *vaen* from the elders... and why. I had never ventured this far from the village before, and the rich smells of the surrounding forest engulfed me. I thought about my father walking this same path as the feathers of his arrows brushed my hand. I quickened my pace and fell into step with Seng.

"Seng, last night at Anok's naming ceremony..." I started. I could see the muscles in his jaw tighten at the mention of his son. "I saw you going to the Elders' hutch... what were you—"

Suddenly, Naav cried out.

"Look!" He pointed, squatting over a fresh set of tracks. We gathered near him to peer at the odd imprints in the soft dirt. Naav frowned as he brushed the earth with his fingers. "Too large for a deer, but..." his voice trailed off. I looked where he pointed out that the prints were deep, sharp-edged, but... wrong. The other men in the group murmured nervously. Maro put his hand on the blade at his hip. "These don't belong to any man," Naav spoke softly, "or any animal I know." Despite the warmth of the day, I felt a shiver run down my back and my skin prickled. It disturbed me to see the men I was with acting so cautiously. Men who had traveled on this path many times. I glanced at Seng. His normally fierce gaze flickered with something else—hesitation? Worry? His eyes darted to the foliage around us, but something in his posture felt... off.

Out of nowhere, a beast crashed through the bushes, screaming with rage. No, not a beast, but a boar. The men moved quickly, leaving me grasping at my father's arrows and desperate to stay out of the way. The boar turned on the closest man, Maro, and struck him in his middle at full speed. Maro fell to the ground, desperately stabbing at the animal with his hand blade. Another member of the group, Alwa, threw a spear at the boar, piercing the tough hide on its flank. The boar turned and its cold, furious eyes set on me, still fumbling to retrieve an arrow to fit into my bow. It charged, and I gave up on the bow, pulling the *khet* from my leather waistband. I braced myself for the impact when the boar screamed once more and thudded to the ground, mere steps away from me.

Seng stood just behind me, lowering his bow. The boar lay wheezing as its life slowly faded.

I was still in shock when I heard Maro cry out in pain as the others rushed to him. He clutched his side, blood oozing from between his fingers. Naav pulled a cloth from his satchel and wound it around Maro's middle, causing him to cry out again.

"We must return now," Seng said. "We will come back for the boar." He and Alwa, the second-largest man in the group, stood Maro up and took one of the injured man's arms each. They carefully placed his arms over their shoulders to help him walk. I was still shivering from the scare, knowing how close I had come to getting injured like Maro. We made our way back to the village at a much slower pace, and I felt relief wash over me as we entered the area of the forest I was most familiar with. Maro groaned and grunted as his blood continued to drip through his wrappings and down his side.

"Tel..." Maro said weakly. I looked at him and he pointed with his eyes at my snare as we passed it. The fox was gone. All that was left was a hind leg, dangling in the air.

IV

As we grew closer to the village, Seng ordered me to seek one of the elders. I ran ahead of the group, relieved to be in a less dense area of the forest. I entered the clearing of our village, startling a few women with their young children as I dashed past them. I caught Moashi as she exited a hutch carrying a bundle of herbs.

"*Moashi!*" I cried out. She turned to me with concern, hearing the panic in my voice. "Moashi," I panted and relayed the message between gasps. "It's Maro. He's been hurt. A boar." She nodded and took my hand, leading me in the direction of the Elders' hutch. She instructed me to wait outside and disappeared through the entrance. She returned quickly, clutching a *vaen* in her hand. On the other side of the village, I heard the cries of others as Seng and the other men returned with the gravely injured Maro.

"Tel," Moashi spoke harshly. "Take this to them. You must hurry!" She seemed so much more frail than she had just the night before. She handed me the *vaen*, and I looked at the small wax-sealed bone in my hand. It was etched with signs and had a small colored string tied around it. I had never held or touched a *vaen* before and I stared at it. "Go!" Moashi urged.

I broke into a run toward the men, clutching Maro's *vaen* tightly in my fist. Seng and Alwa gently lowered Maro to the ground as I approached. I handed the *vaen* to Naav and he placed the small bone in Maro's mouth.

"Bite down," Naav instructed. Maro's eyes rolled back in his head and his mouth remained loose. "Bite, Maro! Quickly!" Naav urged. When Maro did not respond, Seng stepped closer and hit

Maro's jaw with the palm of his hand, crushing the small bone between his teeth. Almost immediately, Maro began to writhe in pain, thrashing his arms and legs as he shrieked in agony. The other villagers gathered around with worried expressions on their faces. Maro clawed at the wrap that Naav had tied around him and tore it off, making terrifying sounds.

My eyes widened as I watched the ragged gash left from the boar's tusk slowly close up. After a moment, he lay still on the ground, panting in quick, shallow breaths, just like the boar had done before it died. Maro's mate, Taaya, rushed forward to be by his side, but Alwa held her back as gently as possible. Maro's veins turned almost black as his chest rose and fell rapidly, his skin paler than milk. Gradually, his breathing returned to normal, and the color of his skin looked healthy once more. Moashi had finally made her way to the gathering and knelt by his side. She brushed the dark, sweat-dampened hair out of his eyes and whispered a few words in his ear. Finally, she stood.

"He needs rest now," she spoke solemnly. "Seng, Alwa, will you take him back to his home?" She turned to Taaya. "Make sure he drinks and eats by sundown. He is very weak."

Seng and Alwa carried Maro's limp body back to his hutch, with Taaya close by his side, tears streaming down her face as she held her swollen belly. She would have their first child within the next moon. The rest of the clan lingered behind, talking among themselves in hushed tones. I saw Renai staring at the blood left on the ground and ran up to her.

"Renai," I said softly. "I've been wanting to speak with you." She looked at me as if she had just been woken, then her expression softened.

"Tel, that was incredible. I saw you leaving this morning and I wanted to wish you luck and bravery, but it seems you didn't need it. I'm so glad you're safe!" Renai spoke quickly. She touched her forehead to mine, and I felt my cheeks grow hot. "When I saw you running out of the forest by yourself, I was so worried," she continued.

I bowed my head slightly in thanks. "Renai..." I struggled to find my words. "I haven't seen much of you since..." my voice trailed off. She cast her eyes downward.

"I know. I'm sorry," she said, fidgeting with her *tonak*. I always admired the way she decorated her leathers with small feathers and colorful beads. "I just felt bad about what happened," she continued. "That night, I was sent to fetch more wood to keep my brother warm, and when I saw you gathering wood for the fires at the same time, I just wanted to speak to you."

I almost smiled, but then I remembered that her brother, Keo, had passed away not long after that night from the burning sickness. He was only 6 when he left us and joined the ancestors. I was at fault too. After Keo died, I kept my distance from her, not knowing what to say at the time. We stood in silence for a moment before Seng's voice cut through the air.

"Tel," he spoke softly, for once. "Come with me." I nodded a quick farewell to Renai and trotted over to Seng, not wanting to keep him waiting. He placed his hand on my shoulder, and I instinctively flinched at the unfamiliar touch. "You were brave today," he said as we walked toward the edge of the village. "You did well," he continued when I said nothing. I nodded solemnly in thanks, still struggling to find my words. "We must retrieve the boar, it will feed many and would be a shame to waste," Seng said finally. I nodded again and we made our way back out of the village into the forest for the second time that day.

V

As we were walking, I found my voice and tried to continue my question from earlier. "Last night I saw you follow Moashi to the elders' hutch," I blurted out. "Why?" I kept my eyes on the trail ahead of us to avoid meeting his gaze. I heard Seng sigh.

"I just wanted to make sure that Anok—" he paused as he said his son's name. My father's name. "I wanted to make sure his *vaen* made it back to the hutch safely." He stopped walking and turned me to face him. His dark eyes locked with my own.

"Your father was my closest friend, Tel. I wouldn't be here if he hadn't saved my life." Seng's strong hands gripped my shoulders. "We were out farther than usual, tracking down a buck that I had struck with one of my arrows," he continued. "The sun was getting low, and your father wanted to give up the hunt and head back to the village. I knew we were getting close and convinced him to keep searching with me just a little longer. We found the deer, but there was something else there too. A creature, feasting on it as it lay helpless, screeching in fear and pain. The creature turned when it heard us approaching." My throat ran dry, and my hands grew clammy hearing this. My mother had never shared the details of how my father died. I'm not even sure she knew the entire truth herself.

"It was unlike anything I had ever seen. It stood like a man, but the legs... bent the wrong way—like a stag, but the flesh was cracked and raw, as if the bone was trying to escape the skin. Horns jutted from the head. Not like an animal's, but more like roots—twisted and jagged, growing from a skull too small to support them." Seng's voice dropped to a whisper as his eyes scanned the surrounding trees.

"The eyes..." he continued. "The eyes were large and dark, like an owl, but dead. There was no life behind them... only hunger."

"The arms and legs were long and spindly, but strong, with claws sharper than a bear or mountain cat. You could see its muscles rippling, even from a distance. I noticed it was missing one of its front paws, but—" Seng must've noticed the clear terror on my face and released my shoulders from his grip to continue walking. As we followed the blood-stained trail, he went on.

"The creature charged at us. Like you today, I struggled to draw my bow in time." Seng scratched at the side of his neck absentmindedly. "Your father, he jumped between me and the creature and was tackled to the ground. He was able to slash at it with his *khet* while they struggled, and I ended it with a single arrow to the creature's heart... but it was too late for your father."

I walked in silence, taking in all this new information. My eyes burned and threatened to start watering from the images in my mind. I was lost in my thoughts when Seng put his hand across my chest to halt me. I looked up. Ahead, I saw the boar from earlier that day, or at least what was left of it.

The arrow still stuck out of the eye, where Seng had shot it, but the body had been mutilated and torn open. Organs were strewn about the small clearing, with hunks of flesh ripped from the body.

"A bear?" I asked, my hand instinctively moving toward the *khet* at my hip.

"No," Seng said. "This was one of them. Those tracks we saw this morning... the same kind of tracks left by the creature that killed your father. We should head back. Now."

I searched the surrounding foliage for any sign of danger as we turned around, but it seemed calm with birds chirping and squirrels bounding to and fro. We walked with a brisk gait, barely speaking until we passed the snare with the fox leg still dangling from it. I pointed it out to Seng and told him about how I saw the fox that morning, still alive, but on the way back, Maro pointed out that it was gone. He nodded in silence and quickened his pace. We reached the entrance to our village just as the sun was starting to fade. I noticed Seng's movements relax once we stepped past the circular perimeter of the fires, which were being lit by other clan members.

VI

I returned to my hutch to find Ulak leaving as I approached. He gave me a quick nod of acknowledgment as he passed by me. I entered, pushing past the deerskin flap to find my mother and

Kuri sitting by a small fire inside. I could see traces of tears on my mother's cheeks, and Kuri looked unusually somber.

"What's wrong?" I asked, kneeling by my mother's side. "Why was Ulak here?" She took a deep shuddering breath and was silent for a while before speaking.

"Ulak's wife was not taken from the village," she said at last. "She fled, after using a *vaen* that did not belong to her. She and Ulak had been trying to have a child, and out of desperation, she thought that a *vaen* might help them. So she stole the *vaen* of Renai's brother, Keo. Ulak found what she had done after she started to... change. Her nails grew long, and her veins and skin grew darker. She began to act like a wild animal." I opened my mouth to speak, but my mother held her hand up to silence me.

"When he tried to leave to seek help from the elders, she attacked him. He could have been killed that night, but she hesitated and ran into the forest instead. He chased after her, but the elders agreed it would be best to let the rest of us believe that the creatures stole her away instead of knowing that she... *became one of them*." I glanced at Kuri, who stared into the fire, avoiding eye contact with me and our mother.

"But why was Ulak here, telling you this?" I asked. My mother nodded slowly, another tear rolling slowly down her face.

"Your grandfather once did the same. Not long after Kuri was born, he began to feel ill more often, weaker. He felt his life slowly draining from him as he aged." My mother continued the story. "He grew envious of Anok, your father, and one night he broke into the elders' hutch and stole his *vaen*, consuming it, as if it would make him young once more." I glanced at Kuri, who looked at me with the same shocked expression.

"He changed into a monster that night. He came crashing into our hutch, and your father fought him off, severing his left hand with his *khet*. After that, your grandfather retreated to the forest and we assumed he would—" she paused for a moment, "... die from his injuries."

I thought of the story that Seng had just told me about my father dying after being attacked by a creature missing a hand. My head was spinning. I stood abruptly. I needed fresh air. My mother called out to me as I pushed my way out of our hutch into the night and started walking. I had to speak to Ulak.

VII

The words of my mother echoed in my head as I made my way towards Ulak's hutch. The light from his fire flickered against the interior of his home, but I paused when I saw two figures inside, speaking in hushed voices. One voice belonged to Ulak, and the other unmistakably belonged to Moashi. I stayed hidden in the shadows between the hutches, listening to the conversation, wondering what other secrets had been kept from me. Ulak sounded bitter and angry.

"You and the other elders should have told them all. Seasons ago." Ulak's voice was clear as he struggled to keep his voice calm.

"And watch the clan tear themselves apart like animals?" Moashi's voice was kind, as always, but firm. "You know what desperation makes of people. You of all men should know." There was a pause before Ulak spoke again. I lingered on every word; my mouth ran dry as I listened to his next words.

"You mean what it made of my mate," Ulak spoke with a gravelly tone.

"Your mate, and what happened to Anok," Moashi said softly. My throat tightened and my stomach twisted as I realized they were talking about my father.

"The truth would not have saved your mate or Tel's father, but it could have destroyed the rest of the clan," Moashi continued firmly.

"So you chose silence over the truth instead?" Ulak spat back at her. His voice was elevated as he tried to maintain composure when speaking with an elder.

"No, Ulak," Moashi said in her unwavering tone. "I chose the living over the dead. The blood is tied to the soul," her voice cold as the river's heart. "A man who steals another's life does not become stronger—he becomes something *else*. Grief makes monsters of us all. If the clan knew this... how long before grief or greed led them to try? You must understand, Ulak. The future of our clan is at stake. You should not have shared that information tonight."

My breath hitched, and I made a small noise, causing Ulak and Moashi to cease their discussion.

"Who's there?" Moashi called out harshly. After I remained silent, she spoke to Ulak again.

"I must go," she said. "Be wary of what you share with others, Ulak."

She slipped out of his hutch silently and headed back to the elders' hutch. I remained as quiet as possible as I watched her go. I was still reeling from hearing Moashi speak so plainly about the devastation that the *vaen* caused to several families in our village when I heard soft footsteps behind me. I whirled around to see no one, but my skin prickled just as it had before the boar attack. I peered out into the dark forest beyond the perimeter fires. Then I saw it move.

I grasped the *khet* at my waist, wondering what could be lurking and watching me. Ulak's hutch was the closest to the treeline, slightly set away from the rest of the village that bathed in the glow of the protective fires each night.

"*Tel*," came a hoarse whisper, barely audible above the crackling fires. Something about the voice sounded familiar to me. With the *khet* firmly gripped in my hand, I stepped past the flames and into the darkness beyond. Despite the fire at my back, I still felt a chill as I crossed the boundaries of the village. I stood motionless for a moment, contemplating the conversation I had just overheard. Then the nearby brush began to move. A dark creature slipped between the branches and approached me slowly, walking on two legs.

"Tel," it said again. The voice was barely recognizable, but I saw the small feathers and beads that adorned the tattered shreds of leather on its body.

"Renai?" I choked out, taking a step back toward the flames. She—*it*, approached me cautiously, lingering in the shadows of the foliage. Her skin was already graying, her once beautiful eyes were dark and too large. Her lips trembled and her teeth... they were *wrong*.

"They said the blood was tied to the soul," she said in a raspy voice. "I thought... If I offered enough—if I gave them the elders' *vaen*, it would be enough for them to bring him back."

"What have you done, Renai?" My voice shook as I spoke, horrified at the realization.

Renai started to shake, her eyes rested on the *khet* in my hand. She lunged at me suddenly, only to be driven back by the glow of the flames. Her eyes flickered with guilt, grief, and something else entirely. Something animalistic. It reminded me of the way that the boar had stared at me with pure hatred before it charged.

"I *heard* him," she spoke again. "I heard Keo, I swear it was his voice, but... it wasn't him. It wasn't my brother who answered my calls." I could see the flames of the fires behind me reflected in her dark, glassy eyes as she spoke to me one final time.

"I'm sorry, Tel. I never meant for you to see me... like this." Her voice was soft, almost like the Renai I knew, then it changed again, and she doubled over, clutching her middle. "Tell them not to come for me," she said, at last, slowly retreating into the darkness of the forest.

VIII

I clapped my hands on my thighs before standing. The children of the village all stared at me with a mixture of wonder and horror in their eyes.

"That can't be the end!" Cried out Ren, my son. He was supported by a cacophony of comments, questions, and complaints by his peers. Ren was just coming into his 6th summer, the same age as Renai's brother, Keo, when he left us.

"That's all for this night," I said, adding a few more logs to the fire.

"Elder Tel, what happened to Renai?" A girl asked.

I shrugged. "Maybe she's still out there... waiting to take children who don't listen to their elders."

Kuri helped me usher the children back to their hutches to join their families for the night. She touched foreheads with me briefly before returning to her mate.

"You honor our past elders with your stories, Tel. Mother and father would be proud of you," she said, before heading home.

I stayed in the silence of the night for a while, embracing the cool breeze on my skin as I inhaled the rich scents from the forest. The moon shone brightly, illuminating the trees beyond the village fires. I was about to head back to my hutch when I heard my name, as if whispered through the wind, and froze. She was still out there, watching and waiting for me.

FAMILY

One

MOSQUITOS AND GNATS SWARMED around Maria within seconds of getting out of her car, as if the southern heat and humidity alone didn't make it hard enough to breathe. Ripley seemed unaffected by these conditions; he was more concerned with sniffing each individual blade of grass before deciding which to mark with his scent. Maria waited as patiently as she could, swatting at the flying insects.

"Come on, old man." Maria sighed. Ripley had finished his business and was now clearly dragging his feet, reluctant to get back in the car after the long ride. She tugged gently on Ripley's leash and he huffed indignantly before allowing her to lead him back to the car. Maria grabbed the passenger door handle to let Ripley in first. It was locked. "Huh," she grunted. Sweat had begun to bead on her forehead. She walked around to the driver's side and tried her door. Also locked. She could see the keys sitting in the center console, peeking out from underneath a crumpled receipt.

Frustrated, she pulled the handles of all the doors, and even the trunk a few times out of desperation.

"No, no, no...!" She groaned. She looked around for any rocks or sticks that might be large enough to break one of the windows. A mosquito bit the back of her thigh and she slapped at it angrily. Ripley stepped back, startled by the aggressive motion and sound. After scanning their surroundings, Maria could see nothing but shaggy grass and reeds along the road. Past them, the land sloped down into a cypress-laden swamp. From the looks of it, there hadn't been any rain in the area lately.

She contemplated poking around near the edge of the receded water line but knew it wasn't safe for her or Ripley. Snakes and alligators like to snooze in the sunlight closest to the edge of the swamp in case they need to make a hasty getaway. Or to prey on any creatures who might venture too close to get water.

Maria swallowed at the thought of water, her throat was already drying up. Ripley was sitting in her shadow, panting. It was barely noon; they couldn't last all day out in the heat. She walked in the direction they were going, considering the road behind them was only hours of Louisiana bayou backroads. Seeing another car on the road had been a rarity the past few hours, so she knew she couldn't rely on someone just passing by.

About a mile later, Maria thought she heard a diesel engine. She stopped to listen, but all the overgrown vegetation and shaggy moss muffled whatever she thought she heard. Her shirt clung to her back, damp with sweat. Even Ripley had lost his interest in sniffing and marking, trudging alongside her with a droopy tail. Maria's tongue and throat felt like sandpaper. She wondered how hot it was, and how long they had before dehydration and heat exhaustion became life-threatening. Not long was her guess.

Ripley kept pulling her toward the shaded tall grass near the edge of the swamp. She knew it wasn't the safest idea, but an aging dog with a black coat roasting in the sun wasn't ideal either. She scooped him up into her arms and stepped off the road. The grass was prickly against her legs, making her aware of how exposed she was to all things that bite and sting. Maria found a small dirt clearing in the shade and put the dog down. He immediately flopped onto the cool earth. She eyed the muddy brown water remaining in the dried-up swamp and wondered if it was even safe for a dog to drink.

She decided a few drops to at least wet poor Ripley's tongue would be worth the risk. She got up and took a few cautious steps towards the water's edge. The heavy smell of the decaying animal and plant matter hit Maria as she got closer. It looked like she would have to walk through a few feet of questionable swamp muck to reach the water. She looked back at Ripley; he hadn't even gotten up to see where she had gone to. She needed to get water for him. She was about to take her first step into the mud when a voice stopped her.

"I wouldn't do that, miss," a heavily accented voice called out behind her. Maria's head whipped around to see a tall man in his late twenties. He was holding a hunting rifle. "That mud don't look deep, but it'll getcha good and stuck. Easy pickin's for the gators." He stepped closer but stopped when he saw Maria staring at the rifle. He slung the gun over his shoulder and raised his hands as a gesture of goodwill. "I don't mean you no harm, miss." His accent was light, just a hint of southern twang. "Just doing some hunting around here and I spotted you about to take a mud bath is all."

"Do you have any water with you?" Maria asked. "I locked myself out of my car and we've been walking..." She pointed at Ripley, without taking her eyes off the man.

He reached down to his side and tossed her a canteen. "I always carry some on me. The heat will getcha, too." He smiled and winked at her, and Maria felt a little more at ease. She thanked him and jogged over to where poor Ripley was. She splashed some cool water onto his face and body, which startled him, but she was glad to see he was still responsive. He lapped water out of her cupped hands and then flopped back onto his side.

"He's awful lucky he's got you around," the man stated, following Maria out from the cypress trees. "But I would save some of that water, we've got a bit of a walk to go still before we reach the house."

"We?" Maria repeated, standing up. She was still wary. He lit a cigarette casually. "Yes, ma'am. You said you were locked out of your car. My house is the only place around for miles. You'll be able to contact someone from there about your car." Maria considered the alternatives. She pictured some run-down trailer home parked somewhere in the swamp.

"How far of a walk did you say it was, Mr...."

"I just go by Joe, ma'am. It's about a forty-minute walk if you cut straight through the bayou. From the looks of your pup and the way you're dressed, though, I'd say it's safer to stick to the roads which'll tack on another twenty minutes."

Maria looked at Joe's attire. He wore dark green coveralls with black rubber boots that came up to his knees. He wasn't much of an eye catcher; he had a plain face and unkempt dark hair. A pink scar trailed down the left side of his face, from his cheekbone to his jaw. A wide-brimmed oilcloth hat sat squashed onto his head, keeping the sun off his face. Compared to her sneakers and shorts, he was considerably more prepared than her for their environment.

"Okay, Joe. Lead the way." She bent to scoop up Ripley, so he didn't have to walk as far.

"You never told me your name," Joe said as they started down the road.

"It's Maria." She thought about giving her last name as well but decided against it. "This is Ripley," she added, at last.

The walk seemed much longer than an hour, and at one point it almost felt like they had doubled back. Ripley grew heavy in Maria's arms, so she let him walk on his leash. Conversation was polite and came in brief clusters of questions and answers. Maria watched Joe as he spoke. Everything he said started or ended with a pleasant southern "miss" or "ma'am," but she felt like he was also concealing something else in his demeanor. She couldn't quite put her finger on what it was, and that bothered her.

As they turned down a wide gravel path, Maria looked ahead and saw a beautiful Southern plantation-style house. The drive was lined with tall oaks draped with scarves of Spanish moss. Large white pillars made the front porch look regal; they reminded Maria of the White House.

"This is your house?" she asked, trying to hide the astonishment in her voice. "It's my mother's," he replied. When he turned to look at her, his eyes lingered a little too long for Maria's comfort. After a short pause, he continued. "At her age, my sister and I thought it best that we stay close to help with the house and property. Always something that needs to get done around here."

Loud baying interrupted Maria's thoughts as a large rust-colored hound came barreling around the corner of the house. Ripley immediately jumped to the challenge and yapped back, tugging at his leash. Despite his bravest efforts, Maria picked him up off the ground as the strange dog continued to approach in an aggressive manner.

"Hey, Roux!" Joe exclaimed, bending over to greet the dog. "This is my sister's dog, Roux. He's a big loaf most of the time, but I'd be careful with your little dog around him. Sometimes he doesn't know his own strength."

Maria felt a little more at ease once she saw the dog respond to Joe's voice and lean against his legs for back rubs, but the way the dog looked at her still made her uncomfortable.

A woman who looked slightly older than Joe appeared in the doorway on the front porch. "Roux, come here, boy!" Roux immediately abandoned Joe to join her side. Her voice was light and melodic. If not for the dirt-stained gardening outfit, she could've been on the cover of a magazine. Putting a gloved hand to her brow, she squinted into the afternoon sun. "Who is our guest, brother?" she called.

Joe turned to Maria. "My sister, Vivienne." To his sister, he responded, "This is Maria, she locked herself out of her car a few miles down Old Parrish Road."

"Oh, dear!" Vivienne exclaimed. "Y'all must be parched, look at your poor little dog! Come in, please. I'll ask Violet to fix you some sweet tea with lemon. Hers is the best in all of Louisiana. Come, come!" She ushered Maria up the steps and into the house.

"I've got some things to wrap up before I come in," Joe remained in the driveway. "Keep a cold one waiting for me, ladies," he added with another wink before walking around the side of the house.

The temperature dropped several degrees once they were inside the grand foyer. Maria's skin prickled at the abrupt contrast, but she was grateful to be inside and out of the heat. "I'll put Roux out back with Joe, so you can put your dog down safely. I'm sure Joe's told you that Roux isn't great with other dogs, especially smaller ones." Vivienne spoke over her shoulder as she took Roux by the collar and led him to a back door. Maria heard her speaking to someone in the kitchen and waited until she saw Vivienne return to respond.

"Thanks, he was getting a little heavy," Maria said as she put Ripley down. He seemed content enough, with a nice cool wooden floor to stretch out on. Vivienne was carrying two glasses of iced tea in her hands. She must've removed her gardening gloves in the kitchen somewhere. Maria thanked her as she took one of the glasses and sipped. It felt like liquid gold as the cold tea splashed down her throat.

"I'll bet your little dog would like something to drink as well. Would you care to join me in the kitchen? Mother hates when dog slobber gets all over her floors."

"Oh, sure. Thank you," Maria responded. "Ripley says thank you, too."

Vivienne chuckled. "Ripley. What a perfect name for him." Maria wasn't quite sure what she meant by that but took it as a compliment regardless. Once in the kitchen, Maria saw an elderly woman bustling about making some sort of paella, by the looks of things.

"Violet, please get a small dish of water for Maria's dog, Ripley," Vivienne said. The airy southern politeness in her voice seemed to disappear for a moment and was replaced with a sharper tone. Violet nodded and immediately stopped chopping onions to find a bowl for water. "Oh, I can do it if she's busy—" Maria started to move but was silenced by a raised hand from Vivienne.

"Violet feels best when she is busy. She enjoys this work, don't you?" Violet said nothing and smiled sweetly as she placed the dish on a placemat. Ripley wasted no time and lapped the water greedily. Vivienne leaned close to Maria and whispered, "Violet is mute. She hasn't spoken a word in forty-four years, or so I've been told. I've only been around for thirty-three of them."

"Why, hello there." A new voice broke the momentary silence as Maria searched for something to say in response about Violet. She turned to see another elderly woman in the doorway of the kitchen. She was in a floor-length dress with sleeves that reminded Maria of a Japanese kimono. A cigarette dangled delicately between the fingers of her left hand, which donned an enormous diamond-encrusted wedding ring. Her fine white hair was swept up and pinned in a perfect French twist. A string of pearls rested on her collarbone, just above where the dress ended.

"Mother, this is Maria. Her car broke down along the road a few miles away."

"Actually, it didn't break. I just locked the keys inside it by accident." Maria corrected. "It's nice to meet you, Miss..."

"Chevalier," the woman replied proudly with a toss of her head. "But you may call me Mother if you like. Everyone else does." Her accent was the strongest, most determinable as people would call "Old South." The way she carried herself and spoke reminded Maria of a movie star from the 40s.

"Maria," Mother repeated. She eyed Maria up and down, making no attempt to be subtle about it. This added to the growing unease that Maria felt in her gut.

"Do you have a telephone I could use to call a locksmith?" she asked.

"Maria is a biblical name, you know," Mother ignored her question. "Not many people realize that. It means 'rebellious woman,' Maria." She continued, "Do you consider yourself rebellious?"

Maria glanced at Vivienne but her expression was cold and detached. She almost looked like a different person from when she greeted Maria on the porch. Vivienne offered no support or rescue from her mother's odd interrogation. Out of the corner of her eye, Maria could also see Violet, peeking at them from behind her cutting board. Heat prickled at the back of Maria's neck; she did not like being stared at. She did not like this situation she had found herself in.

"If I could just use the phone..." Maria began again.

"Oh no, no, no, dear," Mother cooed at her. "We haven't had a working telephone out here for a few years. The lines kept getting torn down by the summer storms. After a while, we just gave up trying, I suppose." It grated on Maria the way Mother pronounced the "h" in while, but that was the least of her concerns at the moment.

"Would someone be able to give me a lift into town, then?" Maria kept at it. "Joe, maybe?"

Vivienne cut in. "You like Joe more than me? Mother, did you hear that? Maria would prefer Joseph drive her into town for help," Maria felt her face flush from Vivienne's accusing tone.

"That's not what I meant," Maria paused. She was sweating again, and she felt unsteady on her feet. Ripley barked and she looked in his direction. Joe had come in through the back door and was saying something to Mother, but Maria couldn't make out his words. She put her hand on the table to balance herself as dark circles swirled in her eyes, giving her tunnel vision.

"Are you feeling quite all right, dear?" Mother asked, stepping closer. She put the back of her hand against Maria's forehead. "The heat, maybe?"

Then Maria was on the floor. It felt like she was underwater, drifting off into a world of muted darkness. The last thing she heard was Ripley's panicked barking.

Two

When she woke it was getting dark outside. She sat up groggily and took in her surroundings. She was in a bed, and the room she was in looked like it was meant for a young girl. The bedding was lavender with small white flowers embroidered on the comforter, the walls were a pale yellow, and there was a bureau with a vanity mirror far too small for an adult to sit at.

She stood up, slightly unsteady on her feet still. On the bureau was a glass of water, a biscuit with a pat of butter, and an old hairbrush with a wooden handle. Maria noticed a small note placed next to the biscuit and picked it up.

When you are finished with your meal, please brush your hair. Someone will be around to collect you shortly.

With love,

Mother

Maria read the note twice before going to the door. She put her ear to it but couldn't hear anything on the other side. She grabbed the doorknob and twisted. It was locked. She tried the sole window in the room, but it wouldn't open more than two inches. Her head was throbbing. It felt like her racing heartbeat was an air pump, slowly inflating her skull until it was ready to explode.

She finished the water in several large gulps, which seemed to help after a few moments. She tried the door again.

"Hey!" She pounded the door with a closed fist. "Let me out of here, you can't lock me in here like this!" She kicked at the base of the door, which did little, but was much louder and easier to continue without hurting her hands. After a while, she stopped and listened for approaching footsteps. When she heard none, she continued her assault on the door, making a ruckus.

When she finally heard a key in the lock, she stopped and backed away from the door. It swung open and Vivienne stood there.

"You haven't touched your food," she observed, speaking lightly. Maria stepped closer.

"What the hell did you put in my drink?"

Vivienne looked shocked. "Why, me?" Her southern accent made her sound almost like a cliché of Daisy Duke. "I wouldn't know the slightest about that, dear. You barely drank any at all before the sweet Louisiana heat got to you. You should be thankful that Mother was such a gracious host to a complete stranger. We locked your door before we retired for the night because Mother has priceless valuables in the house she would miss dearly if you were to make off with them in the middle of the night." Ripley. Maria had forgotten about him in her disorientation.

"Where is he? My dog, where is he?" Maria asked brusquely. Vivienne's words made sense if they were true, but she wasn't certain of that.

"Oh, your Ripley is just fine. I've had to keep him in my room with me to keep him out of Roux's path. He doesn't take kindly to other newcomers." Vivienne's smile was like poison.

"I need to leave. I'm sorry for any trouble I've caused." Maria spoke quickly, desperate to get away from these people.

"And miss out on supper?" Vivienne asked. "Violet's been slaving away on her specialty dish all day—surely you'd like something to eat."

Maria shook her head. "No, thank you. I'd just like to take my dog and leave your family in peace. I'll find my own way."

"I can't imagine you would get very far walking out in the bayou at this time of day. Those mosquitos alone will be the end of you. Come to dinner, or you'll never see that dog again." Her tone was menacing.

Maria sat at a lavishly set table. At the head of the table was Mother. Joe sat across from her in a fresh change of clothing, next to a young woman. She stared down at her hands. A diamond ring on her left hand sparkled in the light, but the fresh bruise on her cheekbone is what caught Maria's attention. Vivienne, who sat next to Maria, leaned in close and whispered to her. "That's Addison, newest addition to our family. She and Joe are fixing to get married in the fall. Isn't that exciting?" Maria wasn't sure how to answer, imagining how that bruise came to be. She nodded simply.

Thankfully, Violet came in from the kitchen then, pushing a cart that held the large pot she had been cooking with earlier. Despite the large knot in her stomach, the food smelled delicious. She realized she had eaten little but a couple of snacks in the car. Another woman, slightly younger than Violet, also appeared from the kitchen, carrying a basket of fresh bread. She approached Mother first but was waved away with a dainty flick of the wrist.

"Angela, can't you see we have a new guest at the table? Manners, my dear woman," Mother tutted.

Angela backed away with her head slightly bowed. "My apologies, Mother. How thoughtless of me." She approached with a smile that made the hair on Maria's neck stand up.

Once the meal was served, Mother raised her glass and spoke. "Thank the Lord for this divine meal we are about to eat. Thank Him for the health of our family, and we ask Him to continue to watch over us as my dear Calvin once did. Amen."

Maria mumbled an amen.

She was hesitant to eat or drink anything these people gave her, but as everybody tore into their bread, dipping the flaky crust into the juices of the tangy paella sauce, she gave in to her hunger.

After a few moments of eating in uncomfortable silence, she spoke. "Thank you, er—Mother, for being such a gracious host." Mother put her fork down and stared at her with a blank expression.

"Think nothing of it, dear. Why, it's almost like you're a part of the family!" Joe and Vivienne chuckled quietly into their meal. Maria looked around, missing out on the joke. Addison was barely eating. Her eyes met Maria's a few times and she looked like she was on the verge of tears. Maria sent silent compassion to her and said nothing else for the rest of dinner, while Joe and Vivienne updated Mother on the daily tasks they were working on that day.

When they were finished, another young woman came to collect their dishes and announce that dessert that night would be banana pudding pie. She bore a striking resemblance to Addison, although much skinnier. She also had a few bruises on her arm that her linen sleeve failed to conceal. She lingered near Addison as she collected her dish and stared into Maria's eyes. Maria could tell what she was trying to say. *Run! Get away from this place!*

"Thank you, Savannah. That will be all for tonight." Mother's voice cut in, breaking up the small moment they shared. Violet appeared shortly with small dishes of the pudding pie while Angela served coffee and tea. Maria wondered vaguely if every dinner was this lavish. She felt guilty for eating it when she saw Savannah peeking at her through the kitchen window a few times, but she needed her strength.

"Maria," Mother started. "Joe will be heading into town tomorrow for supplies and will find someone to help you out with your car. Would you like to help out in the garden while you wait? Think of it as a small token of your appreciation for all that we've done for you." All Maria wanted to do was to get Ripley and hit the road, on foot if she had to, at the crack of dawn.

"Thank you again for all your help and hospitality, but I'd really like to get going in the morning. I'll walk to town myself with Ripley and be out of your hair," she said, politely. Vivienne smirked at her. "Honey, Mother is just being polite by asking. You will help me in the garden tomorrow." She put her hand on Maria's leg.

Maria slapped her hand away and stood abruptly. "No. I want to leave. Like I said, thank you for everything, but I would like to leave. Right now." Addison gasped but everyone else at the table remained icily calm. Mother sipped her tea.

"Go right ahead." Vivienne made a sound of protest but was silenced when Mother raised her hand.

"Vivienne, be a dear and collect Maria's dog for her."

Vivienne shoved herself away from the table and marched out of the dining room. She returned shortly after with Ripley, who was overjoyed to see Maria. She bent to scoop him up as he jumped and slathered her with kisses. She looked around the table and gave another short thank you before turning and leaving, with one last look at Addison. She was relieved, but a little concerned. They had made such a big fuss about her staying only to let her go so easily.

When she stepped outside the night air was cool and reassuring. The moon shone brightly enough for her to see where she was going. She took off at a jog with Ripley at her side toward her car. What a nightmare, she thought. She stopped once, as she got closer to where she thought her car was to pick up a large rock she would use to smash one of the windows in.

When Maria saw the outline of her old Ford Escort ahead, her heart leapt and she ran a little faster. She smashed the passenger side window and reached in to unlock the car, taking care to brush the broken glass off the seat where Ripley usually sat. The engine roared to life, and she whooped triumphantly. She pulled onto the road and continued back toward the Chevalier house. The thought made her anxious, but it was the direction she was headed.

She sped up when she saw the gravel drive she had walked down earlier with Joe. She felt a pang of guilt as she remembered the bruises on Addison and Savannah. She wasn't sure what the full story was, but she knew she had to help them. Her instinct to flee and put as much distance between herself and the house raged internally against her body as she slowed the car to a stop. She had to be smart. She had to have a plan. She pulled a wrinkled handwritten letter out of her glove box and picked at the edges as she read it. By now, she knew it word for word, but it was a good reminder for her of what she needed to do.

Maria drove again, slowly. She was about a quarter of a mile past the gravel drive when she found what she was looking for. A few small shrubs provided enough cover to hide her car behind. Ripley watched her closely as she grabbed supplies from behind her seat and tucked them into her bag. She tried to leave him in the car where he would be safe, but with the window smashed open he just kept jumping out to follow her anyway. In one last effort she tied his leash to the steering wheel, but when she walked away he cried and howled. He would draw someone's attention quickly with the racket he was making. She sighed, slinging her bag over her shoulder. Ripley would have to come back with her. She made sure the doors were unlocked and left the keys in the sun visor and walked back to the house.

Three

She barely reached the end of the gravel drive when she saw a truck coming from the house. She waved and saw Joe behind the wheel when he pulled up beside her. He was dressed in the same hunting gear from earlier. "Hey, Joe," she said, as calmly as her racing heart would allow.

"Maria!" The surprise in his voice was genuine. "I was just on my way to make sure you got back to your car safely." Her eyes fell upon the rifle he had resting next to him on the bench seat. "I apologize about dinner. I know it got a little tense, but Mother means well."

Maria nodded. "I know, and I apologize for my behavior as well. I was just on my way back to ask to stay the night after all. I didn't realize how tired I was, and it seems like I've got a while to go before I reach town."

Joe smiled at her. "Why, of course. Hop in." He grabbed the rifle and put it behind the seats. She got into the truck cab, placing Ripley closest to the door.

She sat close enough to Joe that her thigh touched his. "I didn't realize how chilly it gets out here once the sun goes down," Maria lied. She was anything but chilly at that moment. Joe's lips pressed together, and he said nothing as he turned the truck around to head back to the house.

Right before they got out of the truck, she put her hand on his leg. "I wanted to thank you... for coming out to check on me. Nobody's ever really watched out for me like that before." He looked at her, and she couldn't read his expression. Her stomach twisted. Maybe she had gone too far too fast. He smirked and reached to brush her hair away from her eyes, but pulled his hand back and got out of the truck briskly. "I've got to go let Mother know you will be staying with us after all," he said as he walked away.

Maria didn't see Addison or Savannah anywhere as she walked through the house to get to her room. She could hear Joe's voice somewhere in the distance, talking with Mother. The only person she saw was Vivienne standing in the doorway of the bedroom across the hall from Maria's. "I'll watch your dog for you," she said, taking Ripley's leash out of Maria's hand. Pinpricks of alarm covered Maria's scalp, but she had to be careful. "Mother doesn't like dogs in that room." Vivienne's smile looked venomous, but she said nothing more and retreated into her room. Maria got one last glance at Ripley before Vivienne closed the door. She gulped, worried for him.

Once she got to the room she was previously locked in, she closed the door and put her bag down on the bed. She needed to find the other girls. She was rummaging through her bag when she heard a knock at the door. The door opened without waiting for her response. It was Joe. He leaned against the door frame. "I spoke to Mother, and she said you could stay here but she would greatly appreciate if you helped out in the garden tomorrow."

"Sure, it's the least I could do," she said agreeably. Joe scratched at the stubble around his jaw, lingering in the door. Maria seized the opportunity. "So," she started casually, "How long have you and Addison been engaged?" Joe shrugged dismissively. "Not very long. She's only been around for a few months actually."

"How did you meet?" Maria pressed.

"Oh, I just bumped into her when I was in town. I guess you could say we hit it off. I brought her home for dinner one night to meet Mother. It was Mother's idea, the engagement, but everything just seemed to make sense. Addison is quite…" Maria cocked her head and gave him a small smile. "Beautiful."

She approached him confidently. "And do you love her?" Her fingers brushed against his forearm.

He caught her hand and said, "You've been awful affectionate all of a sudden." Panic rose in Maria's chest as she struggled to think of a response.

He grabbed her other wrist roughly and Maria assumed her plan had failed, but then he kissed her. It was over before she had a chance to react. He pushed her away and walked out. She watched him go for a moment when Vivienne's voice cut into her thoughts.

"My, my… Mother won't be happy if she found out about that. Not to mention his dear fiancée."

"It wasn't anything, please, don't tell anyone. He kissed me, you saw that!" Maria protested, pretending to panic. Vivienne only smiled at her and pulled Maria's door shut. She could hear the key in the lock, preventing her from doing any late-night snooping in search of Addison and Savannah.

In the night, Maria heard the distinctive sound of her door being unlocked. She stayed still and heard the door open slowly and then close. Footsteps followed by the weight of someone sitting at the foot of the bed. A hand gently stroked her leg through the bedding. Maria stirred, acting as if she was just waking up. She looked down to see Joe. "Everyone else is asleep," he whispered. His hand still rested on her knee.

"What?" Maria started, still playing groggy although every cell in her body was being blasted with adrenaline.

Joe's hand crept upward. "No one will hear a thing. Who knows, maybe you could even become my new bride-to-be." Maria glanced at her bag on her bedside table and half sat up, facing him. Despite her revulsion, she spread her knees slightly. He lunged forward abruptly and pressed his mouth to hers. He groped clumsily at her breasts, his motions frenzied. Maria wrapped her legs around his waist and pulled his body to hers. With one hand she grasped at his hair, moving his head to her neck. With her free hand, she reached for her bag. She could feel him pressing himself against her thighs. She just grabbed the handle of her bag to pull it close enough to reach into when he bit her neck.

Maria cried out in shock and his hand flew to her mouth. "Shh! You have to be quiet." He whispered roughly, his face still inches from hers. She nodded vigorously. He sat back and listened for any sounds in the house. When he was satisfied nobody had heard, he pulled his shirt off over his head. He tugged at the shorts that Maria had worn to bed. She began to panic and struggle against him.

"Wait, wait—"

He pulled them down to her ankles and leaned forward again. "You wanted this. I could see it. Why else would you tease me like that?" He ripped her shirt open to reveal her white tank top underneath. His mouth was on her neck again, his hands fumbling to get his belt undone.

She pushed him off with all her strength and dove for her bag. She felt him behind her, pulling her underwear down now. He wrapped his arm around her neck and pushed himself against her again. "So, this is how you want it? Why didn't you just say so?" He growled in her ear. In her bag, her fingers found the object she was looking for and clamped down on it. Joe was biting at her neck again when she swung her arm around and hit him with the taser.

The shock of it caused his jaw to lock down on her as 200 million volts surged through his body. Maria cried out again and jerked away. Joe remained on the bed, still stunned. She grabbed at the wound on her neck and went in for a second round. Joe's body seized again as she stabbed the taser prongs into his thigh. When she was through, she grabbed some rope out of her bag and secured his hands and legs to the bedposts. She tied her ripped shirt around his head as a gag for when he came to. Breathing hard, she listened, as Joe had, for any signs that someone had heard the commotion. When she heard nothing, she grabbed her bag and slipped out into the hallway. She kept her eyes locked on Vivienne's door as she crept past it to continue down the hall. The girls had to be in one of these rooms.

The first one she opened gingerly and saw it was empty. The next door was all the way at the end of the hallway. She grasped the doorknob and tried, but it was locked. She kept the taser gripped tightly in her hand as she crept back to the room where Joe was. He was conscious again by the time she entered the room. His cries were sufficiently muffled by her shirt, but not entirely silenced. She needed to move quickly.

Maria searched his pockets and found a set of keys. She turned to run back to the locked room and smacked into Vivienne. Before Vivienne could say or do anything, Maria gave her a zap with her taser. She stopped when Vivienne collapsed to the floor and ran back into the hallway, stopping only to close and lock the door behind her. She had little time before Vivienne recovered. She raced down the hall with no care for being quiet anymore. Fumbling with the keys, she banged on the door. "Addison? Savannah? Are you guys in there?" She could see the faint light from a lamp appear under the door. When she found the key that fit, she threw the door open.

In the room stood Addison and Savannah, their nightgowns revealed more bruises on their arms and legs. Violet and Angela were also there, sitting up but still in the threadbare cots they each had to sleep in. "What have you done?" Addison started, her eyes darting from the taser in Maria's hand to the open door behind her. Maria ran to her and Savannah and wrapped them in her arms.

"I knew I would find you!" she cried, with tears streaming down her face.

"We'd given up hope that anyone would come for us," Addison said, clutching at Maria. "You're my sisters!" Maria responded. "When I got your letter, I went to the police immediately. They said you two probably just ran off with your boyfriends. When they refused to take me seriously, I had to come up with my own plan."

The doorknob from the room where Vivienne and Joe rattled. "We need to go. Now." Maria said. She looked at Angela and Violet, still on their cots. "Do you want to come with us?" Angela looked tempted for a moment but, in the end, they both shook their heads "no." They didn't have time to argue. Down the hall, they could hear the sound of Joe kicking at the door. It was sturdy, but it wouldn't hold them forever. The three sisters ran down the hall. Maria told them where to look for her car and sent them ahead. She had to get Ripley from Vivienne's room. Thankfully her door was open, but Ripley wasn't in there. The noises coming from Joe and Vivienne trying to get out of the other room had ceased.

There was only one door in the hallway on the other side of the house. It had to be Mother's bedroom. She didn't have to guess once the door flung open and the elderly woman stood there. "What on earth is making all this racket?" She looked considerably less glamorous in the middle of the night. Maria froze. She spoke slowly and carefully. "I came here looking for my sisters. We are all leaving tonight."

Mother smirked. "You're not concerned at all about those two boys that they came with?" Maria hadn't thought about that. She had been so focused on getting her sisters back she didn't stop to think about their boyfriends. Addison was engaged. "They're out in the garden," Mother went on. "We didn't need any new male bloodlines in this family... but we did need some fresh fertilizer. I've never seen the garden flourish so."

A large arm wrapped around Maria's neck from behind. She couldn't see who it was, but she knew it was Joe. She struggled but dropped her taser in doing so. She kicked her legs out and thrashed her arms hoping to make contact with him. Little good it did her; she was already fading into darkness. Her last conscious thoughts were of her sisters, hoping they had made it to the car.

It was barely light outside when Maria woke again. She got up instantly and tried the door. It was open. She walked out into the hallway, suspicious. When she passed by the kitchen, Mother was there sipping tea. "Why, good morning, Maria," she said with sickening sweetness. "I hope you're happy with yourself. Now we find ourselves short on help." Violet stood behind the counter, avoiding Maria's gaze. She could hear Roux baying somewhere outside. Mother clicked her fingernails on the table. "I'm sure you'll fit right in... with the right motivation."

Roux's barking stopped and was replaced by snarling and squeals. A dogfight. Ripley. Maria crashed out the back door to the garden and saw Vivienne and Joe watching as Roux attacked Ripley. The smaller dog fought back for his life as the large hound wrestled him to the ground, pinning him down. Ripley yelped as Roux's jaws clamped down on his back leg. He then shook his head back and forth, whipping Ripley around like he was nothing more than a toy.

Maria cried out, "You savages!" as she ran to her dog. She kicked at the hound's head, viciously screaming at him to stop. He seemed oblivious to her kicks until she landed one on his side, right below his ribcage. He whirled around and bit her ankle. The pain was excruciating, but if Ripley was still fighting, she would too. Vivienne was cackling as Joe moved to grab Maria and drag her away. With her gone, Roux turned his attention to Ripley, who was trying to get a good chomp in on Roux's neck. The rolls of skin and sheer mass made it difficult for the terrier.

Maria watched helplessly as she was hauled away from the skirmish by Joe. When she heard Ripley's squeals end abruptly, she collapsed, defeated. Joe had to drag her dead weight as she screamed and cried for her dog. He dropped her beside the garden fence and squatted to look her in the eye. "You're done now. You've got nothing left. Your sisters are dead." But Maria was barely paying attention. All she could see was Roux bounding up to Vivienne happily, proud of his work. Behind him was a dark mound of fur on the ground. Ripley was gone.

"Are you going to behave now?" Joe continued. "We know from your sisters that your parents are dead. Nobody is going to come looking for you," he sneered. Maria, who was still numb from everything that had happened in the last twenty-four hours, smiled. Joe's expression turned from smug to fury. Seeing this only made Maria chuckle. He slapped her hard across the face. Her response was to burst out in hysterical laughter.

"She's lost it. Seeing her little dog get torn to shreds finally broke that fragile mind of hers," Vivienne said in disgust. Joe stood up and stepped back to join his sister who wrapped her arms around him, leaning her head on his shoulder. Together, they watched as Maria rolled to her side, still laughing uncontrollably. "It's probably best to just cut her tongue out like Violet," Vivienne suggested. "Her mind might be damaged, but her body is not. She can still carry a child."

Maria's laughter died down as she heard something. She giggled a few times, hoping it wasn't her mind playing tricks on her. Maybe she had lost her mind, maybe she was weak. But no, there it was again. A distant wailing, getting closer and louder by the second. Joe and Vivienne heard it now, too; they cocked their heads to the sound of approaching sirens. They had been bluffing. Her sisters made it to the car and were now coming back for her.

"Get her out of sight!" Vivienne hissed at Joe. He moved to pick her up off the ground, but she kicked him viciously, screaming for help. He punched her in the gut, forcing the air from her lungs, silencing her. He grabbed her under her arms and dragged her toward the house. The sirens kept getting louder. She could hear the crunch of the gravel underneath tires. Inside, Mother was barking orders to Violet.

Maria wrenched free from Joe's grasp and took off toward the front of the house. A sheriff, who was just getting out of his car, saw her running towards him and put one hand on his sidearm and held the other out to signal her to stop. She kept on running and screaming for him to help her. When she reached him, he wrestled her to the ground and handcuffed her. "I need you to calm down for me right now," he said. "What is your name?"

Maria was about to answer when Joe interrupted. "Howdy, Sheriff. It's been a while." He smirked at Vivienne, who stood next to him on the front porch. Mother watched from behind them, just inside the open front door. The police officer turned back to Maria. "You just sit tight for a minute; I'll take care of this." He turned back to the Chevaliers. "Hey, Joe. Vivienne. *Madame Chevalier.*" He greeted them jovially with a tip of his wide-brimmed hat. "I picked up two girls speeding on their way to town. They tell me they've been held captive here and that their older sister is still here against her will. How exactly did that come to be?"

"We were caught off-guard," Vivienne spoke. "This one just seemed to fall into our lap and we didn't have much time to research."

The Sheriff pursed his lips at them. "Yes, well. I did my research before coming here," he huffed. "No other living relatives to drop in on you unsuspectingly. I put my neck on the line for your family by not bringing them into the station." Mother clasped her hands and stepped forward onto the porch.

"How thoughtful of you, Sheriff. How can we repay you for your thoughtfulness?"

The Sheriff eyeballed Maria, then looked back at his car. Maria could see Addison and Savannah both huddled in the back seat, looking terrified. He turned back to the Chevalier family.

"I think I'd like to spend an hour with the youngest."

THE LONELY

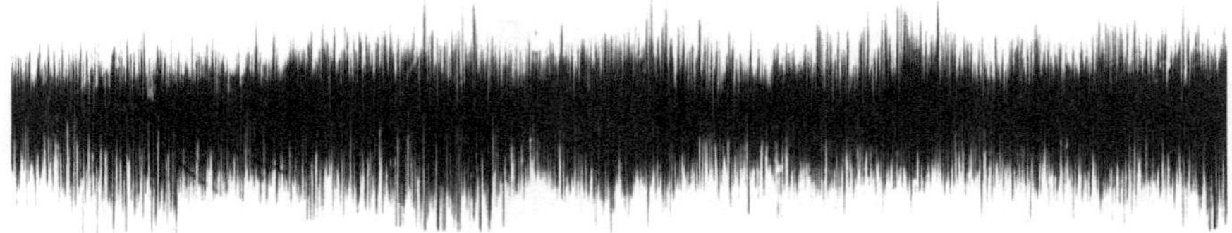

THE LONELY DWELLS IN a dark forest made of the shards of shattered hope. It is summoned by despair and doubt. It does not discriminate who it chooses. The rich, the poor, the young, the old—all have gazed into the Lonely's eyes and felt its dreaded touch.

It wakes to the sound of lovers and friends parting. Breathing in the rich, sickly sweet smell of longing and loss, it slides silently from its lair. It moves in long graceful strides, though it never touches the forest floor.

The Lonely is most active in the darkest hours of the night. It can navigate the tangled undergrowth of abstract thoughts as easily as it drifts through the vaporous mists of memories long gone. It searches, drawn in different directions. It seeks a companion.

Pale, shimmering images of people appear before the Lonely, scattered along its path. Each emits a soft glow from within. It tastes the sadness of their souls as it glides past them. It investigates each figure carefully, lingering with some longer than others. A child sitting by himself at the playground, watching the others play together. An elderly man staring blankly across the table where his wife once sat. A mother whose youngest child just left for college.

The Lonely can tell how badly they are hurting, based on how brightly they shine. It once encountered a man who had just lost his wife and children in a horrific car accident. His pain was so raw and desperate that his light was almost blinding. He had been the one driving. The Lonely spent months with that man, gorging on him.

Each figure also carried a unique aroma that enticed the Lonely. Approaching the silhouette of the young boy, the Lonely can tell he has just moved across country with his parents.

The saltiness of his insecurity made the Lonely salivate in anticipation. It rests its bony hand on the boy's shoulder, curling each finger individually beginning with the pinky. It only touches him for a moment before it retracts its hand in the same spider-like motion. From the boy's shoulder, it draws away a silvery web-like substance. The Lonely beckons to the end of the silky strand with both hands now and it pulls away from the boy, like smoke following a slight draft.

The Lonely gives off a faint glow itself as it inhaled the silvery essence of the boy's sorrow.

In that moment, the boy feels his gut wrench as he watches a group of kids running and screaming, engrossed in an epic game of tag. Inside, he kicks himself for shying away when they had invited him to play. Now, he fears it's too late to change his mind and join them. He pushes the playground mulch with the toe of his sneaker absentmindedly, trying to preoccupy himself with the wonders of dirt and wood chips.

When people feel the Lonely's touch, it carves out parts of them that shape their personality, beliefs, outlook on life, etc. Some release a thin membrane of their former selves, like a snake shedding skin. Others might lose pieces in chunks that fall to the ground and shatter. It depends on how the Lonely sculpts them.

Although it only spends a brief amount of time with each, it leaves a residue on them as a reminder of their time spent together. Like a drop of ink on cloth, the touch of the Lonely stains them.

It slowly spreads, creating intricate and permanent patterns—like tattoos on their souls.

The Lonely senses something savory in its midst and it turns. Hidden eyes scanning from under its dark hood, it searches for the source of the smell and discovers her quickly. A woman. Her glow is faint, but her scent is irresistible. It circles her closely, smoky tendrils of its shroud trailing behind.

The Lonely can see her features more clearly now. As it locks her in its focus, the forest surrounding them dissolves into a black void. Her bright blue eyes were raw in the way that comes from running out of tears before the heart is ready to stop crying. Bits of her apartment come into view as the Lonely slips into her little world. She sits at the edge of her bed, thumbing her phone. Upper Manhattan, New York City. The small clock that sits on her bedside table reads 11:49 p.m. She wears designer yoga pants and a worn-soft t-shirt from her days at NYU, class of '93.

The Lonely watches her as she holds her phone, but she doesn't open it. The unique odor of the woman's sadness washes over the Lonely in delectable waves. It stands directly behind her now and she can almost sense it. The closer it gets, the pitted feeling in her gut worsens and makes her heart ache. It's as if her stomach was a black hole, sucking everything inside of her down into the darkness.

The Lonely reaches out and is just about to touch her when it stops. With its hand lingering in the air just above her shoulder, it recognizes its own mark on her. They had met before. She lost her parents as a teenager years ago when they interrupted a burglary in progress. Two panicked teenagers and a gun they barely knew how to handle.

That night she was staying at a friend's house. The police didn't reach her until the next morning when her parents were supposed to be picking her up. That's how the Lonely found her, a broken child with a glow so bright and the most delectable scent of absolute despair. It spent hours with her over a period of months as she worked through her grief and battled with depression.

The Lonely had danced with her slowly to the sad, mournful music she played. It wrapped its long, dark arms around her, savoring all the emotions that poured out from her core. If it were only possible for the Lonely to experience emotions of its own, perhaps it even enjoyed their time together.

Eventually, she met a boy at one of her grief counseling meetings. Over time her glow became softer, her aroma less pungent. She smiled more often. She spent less time at home, less time *alone*. The Lonely knew that it was time to leave her and find itself another.

"I'm glad you came," she speaks aloud, to her empty apartment. The Lonely withdrew its hand, and she looks back over the shoulder it had almost touched. "It makes sense that you're back now, whatever you are." She opens her phone and plays music over the speakers in her room.

Dark, haunting piano arpeggios rose and swelled in a beautifully sad piece, one that the Lonely was familiar with. This was the song she played countless times after she lost her parents. She even attempted to play the song on the piano at their funeral, but was overcome with emotion and had to stop.

She turned, and for the first time, The Lonely felt a human gaze. It retreated a few steps, unsure of how to react. The woman's eyes were glassy now, and the way they moved made her seem unsure of the Lonely's exact location. She held her hand out in its direction.

"Dance with me again, old friend?"

The Lonely moved forward cautiously, uncertain if she could see it or not. It reached for her outstretched hand. The moment their hands connected, her apartment melted away into a huge, magnificent ballroom. The only light came from a few small candelabras around the room and a single beam of silvery moonlight coming down from above. Deep velvety red curtains draped elegantly from a ceiling that seemed to be miles away.

The piano music swelled, and they danced like they had never before. Her feet left the ground as the Lonely pulled her close and they swept around the room, leaving behind a trail of wispy, silken strands of emotion and energy. She locked eyes with the Lonely as the song slowed. She opened her mouth as if to speak, but no sound came out. Dark black veins spread over her skin, creeping along her arms and up her neck like vines of charcoal. They sank back to the floor, and the Lonely felt her fading.

An icy hand placed itself on the Lonely's shoulder. Death had come for her. Stepping aside for Death to take her in his arms, the ballroom vanished, and the Lonely was back in her apartment. The woman lay in her bed, an empty prescription bottle on the sheets beside her. It looked like she was only sleeping, but the Lonely knew she was gone. Looking at her, the Lonely thought it could feel something. An emotion that came from within. Sadness, perhaps? This sensation only lasted a moment, before it and the Lonely both vanished.

WE

WE ACT DIFFERENTLY WHEN we're around certain people or in various situations. We all do it. Your core personality stays the same essentially, but you act differently with your co-workers than you do with family. Different friends or extended family members get different versions of you. Why are *we* so different?

Jennifer is better at social situations, so she handles those for me. She also takes care of the groceries, because you never know who you'll run into when you're out and about. Once she wasn't feeling well, so I decided I could step up to the task and pick up food for dinner. One of our neighbors was at the store and approached me for some casual chat. I had sweat running down my back by the time the interaction was over. Thankfully I had a jacket on, which covered the sweat stains forming in my pits. I have no logical explanation why I react this way, I just do. That's why Jennifer does the outside stuff.

I'll save you the speculation and a ten-second WebMD search for social anxiety symptoms. My name is Emily, and I have a bad case of agoraphobia. I spend most of my time in my home office, working on my art. You may have even seen some of my work in some of the movie posters from this summer. I won't bore you with my cave-dwelling lifestyle though.

I met Jennifer when I was in high school. Before she came into my life, I was miserable. It's like she breathed new life into my body. She was funny and good at sports. At first, people didn't like her. I guess it's because she was new. You know how high school is. They liked her enough when she won the girl's tennis regionals competition. She became popular enough to be crowned Homecoming Queen our senior year. As her socially awkward friend, I worried that she would be taken away from me with her rising popularity, but she never was. She always included me, made me feel special. I even enjoyed going out to movies with friends and other social events with her... a little.

We ended up being accepted at the same college, so naturally, we lived together. That's when we noticed how different we were. She went out to parties, even on school nights. I would have gone with her, but I had a heavy workload to stay on top of. You can bullshit through an eight-page essay more easily than you can bullshit through art design. The more she partied, the more I withdrew into myself. I got agitated with her more easily. I was exhausted, and she would come home at three a.m., with no regards for my sleep.

One night I snapped at her. She grabbed a few things and walked out the door. I didn't see or hear from her for a week. I was getting worried when she showed up one day and apologized. She said she spent the week at a friend's house and realized that she was being a bad roommate and a bad friend. That she would try to be better, and she did. Our different lifestyles seemed to work themselves out into a decent pattern.

Unfortunately, our newly found equilibrium didn't last long. I was asleep when I heard a commotion in our living room. When I went to see what was going on, I saw a man on top of Jennifer's limp body. They were on the floor near the couch, surrounded by a few empty beer bottles. He had one hand around her throat while the other hand... I can't bring myself to say it. Panic shot up my spine into my skull. I would love to say that I ran to her rescue, but I didn't. I just stood there, paralyzed with fear. I must've blacked out.

When I came to, I was sitting on the couch. Jennifer was crying, but she seemed physically okay. Her arms were wrapped around one of mine and her head was resting on my bicep. In front of us, the man lay on the floor. His throat had been viciously slashed; a broken beer bottle remained protruding from his stomach. I looked down at my own hands and saw they were covered in thick, sticky blood.

I asked Jennifer what had happened. Had I done this? She just shook her head and whispered the name "Doug."

Doug. His name sounded familiar, but I couldn't remember from where. I asked if that was the name of the man on our floor. She scoffed, then told me to think harder.

I scanned through my memories. It was like remembering the melody of a song but forgetting the words and the title and the band. Makes it kind of hard to figure out what that song is and how to find it. A voice in my head told me to keep going further back. I closed my eyes.

When I opened them, my world was entirely black. Almost. As my eyes adjusted to the darkness, I realized that I was in my childhood bedroom. I heard footsteps approaching outside my door and pulled my blankets up to my chin and closed my eyes again. The door opened slowly, and I could hear someone entering the room. My father. I felt the weight on the bed as he sat by my feet. Dread rose up through my body. I felt his hand on my thigh, above the blanket. He never went under the blanket. I could hear what he was doing with his other hand. I just clenched my jaw and kept my eyes shut. A tear slid down my cheek. I felt the groping from his free hand get more frantic before a shaky exhale. He left the room without a word.

Under my bed, I heard movement. A young boy about my age popped his head out. *Doug.* It finally clicked.

"I think we got it," he said grimly, his eyes shining. I nodded. He crawled out from underneath the bed and tiptoed over to my bureau, where he grabbed a teddy bear from the top. He tucked it under my arm and wiped the wetness from my cheek. "I'll stay with you. You'll be okay," he said as he lay down next to me.

The next morning, after my father had left for work, I brought the teddy bear to my mother. She looked at me, confused, before recognizing the bear from my infancy. I didn't say a word, also knowing that when she watched the video on the SD card, she would also see that I had had a boy in my room overnight. I was so worried that she would be angry with me; I was only twelve. I grabbed my backpack and went to school.

When I came home from school, my dad was in the driveway. I bristled instantly, but he didn't even look at me. He was packing his truck. Inside, my mother was crying. When she saw I was home, she ran and wrapped me in a tight hug. She never mentioned the boy in my room. I was grateful.

When I opened my eyes, Jennifer and Doug both sat beside me on the couch. Doug was much bigger now. He had tattoos on his arms and his hair was cropped tight. Much different than the Beiber-look he had when we met. I smiled. The three of us decided what we needed to do, and how we needed to do it. Jennifer called the cops. She spoke to the detectives, to the lawyers, to the court. She broke down in tears during her re-telling of the events that happened. Doug and I were there for moral support, but neither of us had the social skills needed to ensure a ruling of self-defense.

That was years ago. Doug is actually quite funny, but he can get into trouble sometimes. We have to make sure he knows when we have company coming over. Jennifer brought a new guy home once and, as sweet as he was, Doug must have had a stern conversation with him at one point. He didn't come around after that. Jennifer tells me sometimes that when she's out and about someone will ask her "Aren't you afraid of living all by yourself as a woman?" She tells me she smiles at them and answers simply: "We don't."

NEWTON'S THIRD

"YOU HAVE TO COME over today after school. I have something crazy to show you!" Tom said excitedly. I eyed him with suspicion before biting.

"What, did your dad get you the new PlayStation or something?" I asked.

"No, it's not a video game thing. I don't know how to describe it, though. It's like, insane. A *phenomenon.*" He wiggled his fingers like a magician at me. I rolled my eyes.

"Okay," I said. "Let me text my mom to see if I'm allowed." I slid my Blackberry out of my pocket and typed with my hands under my desk. It was still homeroom, but phones weren't permitted to be used during school hours, not even lunch! The phone Nazis were always watching... My phone buzzed a few minutes later with my mom's response. I looked at Tom and grinned.

"She said to just take your bus home with you and she'll pick me up later."

Tom grinned back. "Sweet."

"Derek," Mrs. Hollett scolded me. "Put that away or I'm taking it."

As we boarded the bus, the old man charged with chauffeuring thirty kids to and from school each day put his hand out and stopped me.

"You're not supposed to be on this bus," he said, which sounded more like *"Yer not s'pose to be on thess bus"* in his old-timer Pennsylvanian accent. I glanced at Tom.

"My mom told me I was supposed to ride home with Tom today because she won't be home from work until later." I shrugged.

"She's supposed to tell the school so they can give you a note. You're supposed to have a note; otherwise, I can get in trouble," the old man gruffed. "It's a new policy this year."

"I can show you her text message, or I can call her…" I sputtered, but the bus driver just waved his hand at me dismissively. The buses ahead of ours were already pulling out of the parking lot.

"Go on. Just make sure you have a note next time," he said, putting the bus into gear. We shuffled down the aisle and found two open spots across from each other.

"So, what's this crazy thing you have to show me?" I asked Tom as we got settled in.

"OK. So, I was messing around with a tennis ball yesterday, just tossing it around the basement and it bounced up and hit the top corner of the wall and landed on the couch," Tom started.

"Sounds fascinating already." I put my hands to my cheeks in a "shocked Shirley Temple" pose.

"Then the ball started to float," he continued. I squinted my eyes at him as he went on. "It just popped up off the couch and hovered for a few seconds about chest high before it dropped back to the couch."

"Okay, so your tennis ball hovered for a bit. Did you get a video of it?" I asked, somewhat more intrigued.

"My phone doesn't have a camera… but yours does." Tom raised his eyebrows at me.

"Oh, I see, taking advantage of your poor friend to use his camera phone." I pretended to be hurt as I fished the shiny new Blackberry out of my pocket.

"Hey, I'm the poor friend here," Tom shot back. "I'm lucky my parents got me a phone at all, even if it is a brick," he tapped his Nokia against the bus window. "Anyway, I threw the tennis ball around a few more times, trying to get it to float again. It took me a few minutes to realize that it had to hit the same area on the wall each time."

"Very scientific of you," I stated, rubbing the peach fuzz on my chin. "One phenomenon isn't enough—it has to be repeatable."

We walked to Tom's house from the bus stop, chatting excitedly about different theories that would explain the floating ball. His mom was at the kitchen table on her laptop when Tom and I strolled in.

"Oh, Derek, how nice to see you. I had no idea you would be paying us a visit today..." She gave Tom a look. I gave her a quick greeting and we scurried down into the basement.

"Are you ready?" Tom looked back at me. I was holding my phone out in front of my face. "Yep."

"Okay. This is March 11th, 2006. My name is Tom and recording this is Derek. We are in the basement—"

"Dude, just throw the ball." I cut him off. "Video takes up a lot of memory space."

He nodded and tossed the ball at the spot on the wall. It bounced off and landed on the couch. We watched and waited for a few seconds before I scoffed.

"Coooooool," I said in a bored voice. Tom shushed me and pointed at the ball. It wasn't floating, but it was moving. I stepped closer to get a better shot. The ball lifted up two or three inches, then two feet. It rotated in the air like it was spinning on an axis, making several sharp twists before falling back to the ground and bounced to our feet. Tom and I looked at each other in amazement. He said the ball had never moved in any direction other than up and down before. We took turns throwing the ball at the wall, harder and harder. Each time, the ball would be tossed back at us with matching speed. Once it flew so fast it left a red mark on Tom's arm where it hit him.

"I have an idea," Tom said, sprinting back upstairs. He returned moments later with an apple. We already discovered that the ball didn't have to land on the couch after touching the wall. It just had to touch the wall. He stood on the couch arm and pressed the apple against the spot. "The wall feels kind of warm," he said over his shoulder.

"Maybe that's because we've been slamming it with a rubber ball for the past hour," I suggested. Tom went to place the apple on the couch, but I stopped him. "Wait," I said. "Just hold it out in your hand. Let's see what happens."

He held the apple in an open palm with his fingers flat. He looked like he was trying to feed it to a horse. His arm twitched slightly.

"I can feel the apple moving!" Tom exclaimed. Then the apple was in the air. It looked like Tom was the one making the apple float. "We need a video of this," Tom whispered. "Nobody will believe it!"

As I frantically deleted texts and files to clear space for a new video, the apple lost a chunk of its flesh. It didn't fall to the ground. It just... disappeared. As if something had taken a big bite out of it. Tom stepped back and we watched in silent awe as the rest of the apple quickly disappeared in the same fashion, core and all. I walked back to the couch and waved my hands, half expecting to touch something in the air.

"That was freaky," I said, breaking the silence.

Tom remained quiet for a long time. "I have another idea," he said in a hushed tone. "My sister has a pet guinea pig." I looked at him in horror.

"Dude, no way. What if this thing eats it, too? We have no idea what it is! We should just stick to tennis balls and fruit offerings.

Maybe a banana next. Will it peel it, or just eat the whole thing again?" I was trying to distract Tom from the awful idea of using the guinea pig as a... well, as a guinea pig.

"Okay, okay, you're right. That might get a little too gruesome," Tom said at last. Though I wasn't convinced that he wouldn't still try it on his own after I went home. "How about this? We push record on your phone. Push the phone against the wall, and then leave it on the couch," he clapped his hands and spread his arms out as if he had just pitched a million-dollar idea.

"What, so we can watch a video of ourselves watching my phone?" I questioned him. "Also, what if whatever that *thing* is decides to snack on a fresh juicy Blackberry? It clearly enjoyed that apple."

"That's a risk for sure, but you have insurance on that thing if it gets lost or stolen, right? It's not like your parents wouldn't just get you a new one if you told them someone stole it..." Tom argued back. "But what if your phone's camera can see something we don't?"

"It doesn't," I said, still clutching my phone protectively. "Or we would've seen it in the other videos."

"Your phone never touched the wall—maybe that's the difference. Or maybe it will pick up some audio at least." Tom was persistent. "This could be the first line of real communication. We could be famous for discovering this! Do it for science! You know I would do it if my phone had a camera." I sighed and shook my head.

"All right, but I'm doing it." I hit the record button on my phone and pressed it camera-first into the wall. Then I gingerly set it down on the couch. "Please be very gentle with this. Very careful." I said out loud, just in case.

Tom and I stood back and watched as the phone lifted into the air as delicately as I had set it down. The phone turned in the air and was facing us, then back in the other direction. I felt myself growing tense, waiting for something to happen.

"Derek?" Tom's mom called from the top of the stairs, making us jump. "Your mom is here...!" I let out the breath I didn't realize I had been holding. My phone was still hovering above the couch. I glanced at Tom. He shrugged as if to say, "I don't know what to do." I reached out for my phone.

"I need this back now," I said loudly and clearly, inching closer. The phone looked like it was vibrating in the air now. I grasped it and gave it a gentle tug. It wouldn't budge. The air around the phone felt remarkably warmer than the rest of the cool basement. I shot another look at Tom and got a better grip on my phone and pulled harder. The screen cracked and my hand felt like I had just grabbed a hot pan out of the oven. I fell backward, clutching my hand. As I inspected the area that felt burnt, my phone whipped across the room at me. It made hard contact with the bridge of my nose. It wasn't forceful enough to break it, but it made my eyes water. I grabbed my phone, which was still warm, and stood up.

"Don't mess with this thing anymore, Tom. I'm serious. It seems dangerous." I warned him as I made my way to the stairs. He protested about science and discoveries, but I cut him short. "I think you should show your parents, otherwise... stay out of the basement. Leave it alone." For once, Tom said nothing and just looked back at the wall. I grabbed my backpack and left. That was the last time I saw him.

His mother was the one to find his body after I had left. Naturally, she thought I had done it. I would catch my own parents, who said they believed I didn't do anything, staring at me like I was crazy. Tom couldn't have ripped himself apart and tossed his limbs around the basement. There were also several chunks of him that were never found. The police wrote that up as "Potential Cannibalism." They tested the contents of my stomach. They pulled dental records to compare against the marks left on Tom.

All the while I tried my best to explain to them what I assumed happened to Tom *after* I left his house. They confiscated my phone and dissected everything it contained, which I thought would make my argument that "the invisible thing on the couch" must have killed Tom. I begged them to let me see the footage from the last video I recorded. They asked me questions about things like how we made the tennis ball float, who was the third person who was holding the phone for the last video. They were so sure of themselves, and I was sounding crazier by the minute.

They kept insisting there were more people in the basement. They said that they heard the other voices, the laughter, the music. Even Tom's mother seemed baffled by that. She had already stated that Tom and I were alone downstairs that day. The police would either have to let me go soon or send me to some institute. I could tell they were getting frustrated. They ended up releasing me when they couldn't find a shred of evidence to hold against me. My parents had already sold our house. They said we would have to start fresh somewhere else, where this shadow couldn't lurk over our heads.

On moving day, Tom's mother stopped by. She spoke quietly with my mom in the kitchen. I assumed they were talking about me because they stopped as soon as they noticed me. Tom's mother was in tears.

"Derek, honey. I know you didn't do this. I'm so sorry for what I've put you and your family through, but please, *please*, is there anything else you can tell me about what happened?" I told her the same story I had told my own parents and the police, and the several psychiatrists I had seen. Tom's mother shook her head and turned to leave. "Thank you, Derek."

"Wait, Mrs. Casey," I called out. She turned, her eyes pleading with me. "I know that story sounds insane, that's why we were videotaping it. You can even try it. Just take a tennis ball and throw it at that corner of the wall behind the couch. It will move. See it for yourself, and then leave that basement and never go back down there. Something *is* down there, but the wall is the important factor in getting its attention, I guess. Just leave it alone after that. That's the last thing I said to Tom." She nodded and left.

A few weeks later, we received a phone call from our old town's sheriff's department. My mom answered and put the speakerphone on.

"Ma'am, I'm sorry to bother you, but I thought I should let you know that Mrs. Casey was found dead in her basement. No signs of physical trauma, just a strange smile on her face. I wanted to apologize on behalf of this department for the inconvenience we caused to you and your family during our initial investigation. We will continue our search for the perpetrator, but your son is clear. You and your family take care now."

A MOTHER'S LOVE

CATHY ADJUSTED HER GRIP on the dogs' leashes. Ahead she saw her two sons, pedaling hard on their Huffy bikes. Michael, almost ten, was a few yards ahead of Jamie, who was only six years old. Jamie had just graduated from kindergarten a few days earlier and was relishing the sweet release of summer vacation after a hard first year. The shiny red bike he rode on was his "graduation gift," the first bike he had without training wheels.

Cathy smiled, remembering how she worried about Jamie's reluctance to trade in his training wheels for a big-boy bike. He had clung to his pacifier until he was almost four, only to immediately pick up the habit of thumb-sucking. It was always a battle to convince him that change could be a good thing. He was always more content with the way things were at the moment—even to the point where the doctors had to chemically induce labor after his nine-month lease had come and gone. She loved her firstborn Michael with all her heart, but Jamie was special.

They were taking their regular evening walk along the Greenway trail that ran through their neighborhood. The dogs strained against their leashes to keep up with the boys, but Cathy was determined to walk at her own pace. It was a difficult task to do with dignity, as both dogs were mixes of large breeds. The people at the adoption clinic told her they were both shepherd blends, and she wondered what they were mixed with. Huskies probably, or some sled dog, based on how much they seemed to enjoy pulling at their harnesses.

The boys, who zipped ahead easily on their bikes, circled back on the path to check in with her for what must've been the tenth time since they had turned back towards home. Cathy could see another woman walking a small dog on the trail in the distance, coming her way. She knew the strange dog would be irresistible for her two mutts, Boomer and Ziggy, and was already wrapping their leashes around each hand in preparation for the double-shoulder dislocation that always came with meeting strange dogs on a walk.

"You boys can go ahead if you want and head on home," she said to them. "As long as you promise to stay together and be careful near the road," she added.

"We will be, Mom!" Michael called over his shoulder, already racing off. Jamie pumped his legs, struggling to keep up with his older brother. Cathy smiled to herself, remembering what it was like to be the younger sibling.

The dogs heard something off the trail and barked and pulled aggressively at their leashes. Cathy had to put all of her weight into keeping them by her side. When they finally calmed down, she was out of breath and out of patience. "Come on," she said. "We're going home now."

They were well-behaved for the remainder of the walk, aside from the small dog they terrified. When she got home, she saw her husband Daniel's car parked in the driveway. Jamie was playing in the front yard when he saw his mother approaching with the dogs.

"Mom, you made it!" he announced cheerfully.

"Where's Michael?" he asked, after hugging her legs.

Cathy looked at him. "He didn't come home with you?" she responded, slightly alarmed.

"We heard you calling for him. We were almost home, so he let me go by myself because I'm *big* now," Jamie added proudly.

"Me? I didn't call him back, honey. Where did he go?" She knelt down to look at his face when he answered.

"We both heard you, Mommy. You said you needed help with the dogs, so he went back to help you," Jamie responded, uncertain.

Dan came out the front door with a half-eaten turkey wrap in his hand. "Hey, where's Michael?" he asked before taking a bite.

"I thought he was with you," Cathy fought to stay calm. No need to panic just yet. Maybe Michael just got distracted by one of his friends. She looked around the neighborhood, but there were no other children out playing in their yards. "Michael?" She called, her voice sharp with worry. She turned to her husband.

"Can you call the Sullivans and see if he's there with their boys?" Daniel nodded and ran inside to get his phone.

"Mommy?" Jamie asked. "Where's Michael?" Cathy unleashed the dogs and scooped him up off the ground. He was almost too heavy for her. "I don't know, sweetie. We're looking for him right now." She carried him inside as if she was afraid he might vanish into thin air if she wasn't holding him tightly. Daniel was on his phone. "The Sullivans haven't seen him. I'm trying the Pearsons now." Cathy felt her throat tighten as she listened to Daniel's conversation with Janet Pearson. No sign of Michael.

"Do we call the police?" she asked when he hung up. "We have to give it some time. It's only been what, twenty minutes or so?" He was getting frustrated, too. Jamie watched them silently. His thumb had found its way to his mouth, a habit that only resurfaced in stressful situations.

"You two stay here in case he comes home," Daniel said. "I'm going to drive around and see if I can find him." They kissed before he went out the door.

When Daniel returned two hours later without Michael, they called the police. A squad car with two uniformed officers showed up within a half hour. They asked a lot of questions and took one of Michael's most recent school pictures. They asked Jamie what he had heard, and he told them the same story about hearing Cathy's voice calling Michael back. They asked him multiple times if he saw the woman. *The woman.* Cathy's brain repeated those words repeatedly in her head. She tried to brush away the horrible thoughts hijacking her train of thought. Just last week she had read an article about a woman who had killed her infant in a postpartum rage, only to abduct another child from a playground to fill the void she had created in her life. No. She wouldn't allow herself those thoughts.

The police were unhelpful, saying they could do nothing at this time with no eyewitnesses to give a physical description. She doubted they even believed what Jamie had told them. That night Cathy stayed up next to the phone as long as she could before her need for sleep took over. She woke up to knocking on the front door. It was still dark outside. "Daniel!" She yelled for her husband as she bolted to the door. She could hear him upstairs stumbling around when she yanked the door open and gasped.

Michael was standing in the doorway, covered in thick, black mud. Other than that, he seemed okay. "Michael! Sweetie, where were you? Oh, you had us so scared!" She wrapped her arms around him, tears rolling down her cheeks. Behind her, Daniel cried out when he saw his son home safe and in the arms of his mother and rushed to join the embrace. "Daniel, he's freezing. Can you run a hot bath for him?" She ran to grab blankets off the couch to wrap around Michael as Daniel jumped to the task. When she turned around, she was surprised to see him still lingering in the doorway.

"Honey... come inside so we can get you cleaned up."

Michael stepped forward and Cathy wrapped the blanket around him. She looked at him more carefully now, brushing his hair out of his eyes. "Are you okay?" she asked, studying his face. He only nodded, which concerned her even more as Michael was usually the chatterbox of the house.

"Mommy?" Jamie's voice called from the landing at the top of the stairs. "What's going on?"

She turned to face him. "It's okay, Baby. Michael is home safe now, go back to bed."

Jamie pointed behind her. "Who is that?" She looked back at Michael, but it *wasn't* Michael.

His eyes drifted apart as his face spread into a wide, toothy grin. Cathy stared in horror as he twisted and stretched into this disfigured version of her firstborn. "Get out!" She shrieked as black mud oozed from his mouth. Still smiling, the creature replied in a voice anything but human.

"But Mommy, you told me to come in." Its head shot back, and it opened his jaw and spewed more of the putrid black mud into Cathy's face. She clawed at her face and neck, trying to scrape it off. She could hear the creature cackling and Jamie whimpering behind her. She wanted to run to him, to comfort him, but she felt herself falling. Sinking down into darkness. She called out for Daniel, but her voice echoed like she was in a cave.

Cathy stood in what seemed to be an endless dark void. The only source of light came from high above her. "Daniel! Help me!" she cried again.

"Mommy?" A voice came from behind her. She spun around to see Michael. *Her* Michael, standing behind her. His eyes were red and puffy. Cathy ran to him, but hesitated before hugging him. She reached out and tentatively touched his face. "Is it really you?" she asked.

"Of course it is, Mom," Michael answered, tears welling up in his eyes. "Why did you do this to me?" She wrapped her arms around her son for the second time that night, sobbing.

"What happened to you, Baby?" she finally said.

Michael stepped back from their embrace. "Me and Jamie were almost home, and we heard you calling for me. You said you needed help with Boomer."

Cathy's blood turned to ice as she listened to his words. "Honey—that wasn't me, I didn't call you."

Michael said, "But it was! I saw you in the woods. You threw up on me!" He wailed as he recalled the event. "Then I was home... kinda. I screamed and yelled, but you couldn't hear me down here."

A sudden loud voice grabbed their attention.

"Babe, is everything all right? I heard yelling and Jamie came running for me." Daniel's voice was echoing all around them.

"Help us! Daniel!" Cathy screamed. "Everything is just fine," her own voice calmly spoke over her screams. The light above them shifted, and she realized she could see Daniel's face looking down at them from what felt like miles away. That thing had taken her shape.

"Where is Michael?" Daniel asked, clearly surprised by her sudden calm demeanor. Through the creature's eyes, Cathy could see Jamie, still upstairs, peeking at them from around a corner. "Michael is home safe now. I'm just so glad he's home." The Cathy-creature hugged Daniel, who was uncomfortably confused. Cathy felt sick hearing her own voice lying to her husband, knowing she could do nothing.

"But where is... let go, Cathy. Where's Michael *now?*" Daniel's voice became disgruntled as he struggled against the creature's grip on his torso. "What's the matter with you?" He became increasingly forceful, using his arms to push the creature off. He opened his mouth again to say something and more of that black sludge hit him in the face.

"Daniel!" Cathy screamed, horrified. Michael cried beside her. Shortly after, they heard something moving in the darkness behind them. Daniel appeared, sputtering and wiping at his face. When he saw them, he just stared in shock.

"Dad!" Michael cried, racing over to him. Daniel scooped his son up with a dazed look on his face.

"Cathy?" he said, quietly. "What the hell is going on?"

"I don't know. Whatever that thing is, it can take on our appearance and mimic our voices. It got Michael first, pretending to be me. Then came back for the rest of us." The three of them turned to look through the creature's eyes.

"Jamie!" Daniel said hoarsely. The creature was walking up the stairs. They could see Jamie's head disappear behind the doorway he was peeking from.

"Run, Baby, come on. Go find help. Get out of the house!" Cathy urged him, helplessly watching her youngest son being stalked.

The creature followed Jamie into the room and looked around. He was nowhere to be seen. It crouched down and discovered him hiding under his bed. Tears streaked his little cheeks. Cathy hugged Daniel and Michael, as they all watched in horror. "We'll all be together soon. We can figure this out together, as a family," Daniel said reassuringly, mostly to himself. They all braced, waiting to see the black mud splatter on Jamie's face. Instead, they saw a large hand extend to him. Daniel's hand.

"Come here, champ. It's okay," his voice boomed around them. They watched Jamie as he tentatively took the hand. "Where's Mommy and Michael?" His voice was shaky. "Your Mommy couldn't handle losing Michael, so she ran away. It's just the two of us now, right?" Cathy's stomach sank as she listened. The Daniel-creature continued. "Just remember that they are always with us, here." The hand pointed at Jamie's heart. Jamie still looked uncertain, but nodded anyway.

"No, no, no!" Cathy yelled as she ran, kicking and swinging at the darkness, but to no avail. There was only never-ending emptiness for her to hit. "You can't keep him!" She sank to her knees, hammering the ground beneath her.

"People are going to come and ask us what happened, and that's all you have to say."

The first few days, they tried relentlessly to reach out to the dozens of police officers and family and friends who came by to give condolences. Once they realized it was no use, they sank into quietness. Over the years, Cathy, Daniel, and Michael watched as Jamie grew. Conversations between them grew sparse and eventually stopped altogether. They tried walking to find the end of the void, but it just went on and on. They grew weak, only able to sit or lie down in silence.

Cathy remembered seeing Jamie leaving for college and finally allowing herself to sleep, knowing he had his own life to start now. In a way, she was glad the creature hadn't consumed him. It was selfish of her to want him there with the rest of the family in this dark purgatory. Living there had changed them. Cathy barely even recognized her husband or son anymore. Their faces became gaunt. Fingers and limbs seemed exaggerated. Their skin slowly turned as black as the world they lived in. She closed her eyes for the last time.

A strange sound jerked her back into consciousness. She opened her eyes and was blinded by a brilliant light. She raised her hand to shield her eyes, then realized she had no hand. No limbs. Her body was gone. *Am I a ghost?* she thought. That same noise came again, and she realized it was a squirrel, rustling through some dry leaves. She was in a forest. Then she heard children laughing. She followed the sound and found herself not in the middle of a forest, but at a park.

She watched the children and their parents running about,chasing each other around the fenced-in playground. The sight made her happy at first, but the more she watched, the more she wanted that life back for herself. The life she was robbed of. *She* should be out there watching and playing with her children and her husband. She moved closer but was burned the second the sunlight directly touched her. She would have to stay in the shadows.

She watched one boy in particular for a few moments. His mother sat at a bench on the opposite side of the park, reading a book. The boy wore a red shirt and had a small whistle dangling around his neck. Cathy laughed as she overheard bits and pieces of his dialogue with the other boys.They were playing a pirate game, searching for treasure. He reminded her so much of Jamie and her heart ached. *Robbie*. The name came to her as he got closer to the fence separating them. The fence had a small gap near the bottom. A boy his size could crawl through it easily.

"Robbie?" She called out, not even knowing if she still had a voice. The boy froze. His playmates scampered off, continuing their search for the buried treasure. But he had heard her. "Robbie, can you come here for a second?" Cathy said. She would have her family again. The boy peered into the trees, "Mom? Is that you?"

UNREST

Eric's hands shook as he placed them on the keyboard. The curtains in his dingy studio apartment were drawn, allowing only a thin slice of daylight to score his carpeted floor. He wanted nothing more than to wrap himself in his blankets and go back to sleep, but he had to finish. He was a writer—and his latest work was killing him. Strange things had started happening to him the moment he started his new book, and he was convinced that the only way to end it was to finish the story. At first, he barely even noticed it. A book on his table would be moved a few inches. A pen, previously stationary on his desk, would suddenly roll off and tumble to the floor. He thought nothing of it—barely noticing between cigarette drags and feverish typing. When cabinet doors and drawers started swinging open and slamming violently, he was admittedly spooked. He began to tape them shut, which seemed to work.

Soon he began to feel a distinct presence with him in the apartment, growing stronger with each word he wrote. It was like someone was breathing down his back, looking over his shoulder as he worked. It kept him from sleeping. Even with every door, drawer, and cabinet in his home secured with duct tape, he could hear it rattling them at night. Once he found a large carving knife embedded in his kitchen floor, several feet from its home in the knife block. It scared him enough to rent a room at a nearby motel.

That decision sparked the worst yet. He had barely unpacked his things before a bedside lamp flew past him and crashed into the wall. The bed shook so violently it dislodged the backboard from the wall. The room's phone rang, and Eric picked it up, expecting it to be the front desk asking if everything was okay. Instead, it was a strangely deep voice he had never heard before and hoped to never hear again. It repeated the same thing—whispering over and over. *"Finish it."*

That night he returned to his apartment and continued working, stopping only for a quick bathroom break or a coffee refill. He could feel the presence growing restless and impatient when he paused his writing too long. No time for writer's block. It was going on thirty-six hours and Eric was a wreck. His own reflection gave him a shock during one of his brief bathroom breaks. His eyes were dark and sunken in, and pale skin was drawn tightly over his skull. He looked like a corpse. Perhaps he already was one. Dead in his apartment—held captive in purgatory over an unfinished story.

He was on the last chapter of his story, only a few pages left. Crumpled papers from his notebook strewn around his workspace began to rustle, blown by angry gusts. He cracked his knuckles, trying to figure out how to end it. His hands were pale and bony. He typed something, then immediately deleted it. He sat—hungry, tired, and frustrated. The cabinets were starting to rumble, and he could hear the agitated presence darting around his apartment. A low moan began as it swept invisibly around him, whipping the papers off the floor into the air. He closed his eyes and listened. The moaning grew louder and louder. He took his hands off the keyboard and folded them in his lap. A framed picture flew off the wall with a crash and he barely flinched.

The presence was howling now, and he could feel icy hands clawing at him. He realized now how to end it. He walked calmly over to the shattered frame and picked up a shard of glass.

After neighbors called several times to report a foul smell, Jared, the landlord, investigated the apartment on the third floor. The tenant was always quiet and paid rent on time. Jared hoped everything was okay. As he got off the elevator, the smell hit him and his stomach turned. He knew he should probably call the police then and there, but something made him wait. He knocked twice before using his key to open the door. A wave of decay and death hit him with enough force to make him step back. He peered into the dark apartment from the hallway, holding his hand over his nose and mouth. In the light from the hallway he could see a small wooden table with a laptop and neatly stacked papers. He fumbled for the light switch. When the room lit up, he went pale.

Compared to the neat and orderly desk, the rest of the room was a disaster. It looked like a tornado had blown through the small apartment. Despite all the garbage and destruction, he couldn't locate the source of the smell. Gingerly, he stepped around empty food containers and broken glass and made his way to the bathroom. The door was slightly ajar, and the smell was only getting stronger. He clenched his jaw to brace himself and pushed the door open. Eric, the tenant, was sprawled in the bathtub. His head was rolled back, and his jaw was hanging open. His arms were sliced open from wrist to elbow; blackened blood pooled below the hand that hung over the side of the tub, still clutching a jagged piece of glass.

Jared's eyes watered and he knew he was about to get sick. He stumbled back into the living area, bumping into the desk. He grabbed the table to steady himself and saw a stack of papers had become disturbed. It looked like some kind of manuscript. The front page read:

My Battle with Depression and How I Won
by Eric Monello

Curious, he paged through the loose sheets. Towards the end, the writing became more frenzied and erratic. When he read the last lines, a shiver ran down his spine.

I have depression but it doesn't have me. It will never take me. I won't let it. It will never take me.

IT WILL NEVER HAVE ME.

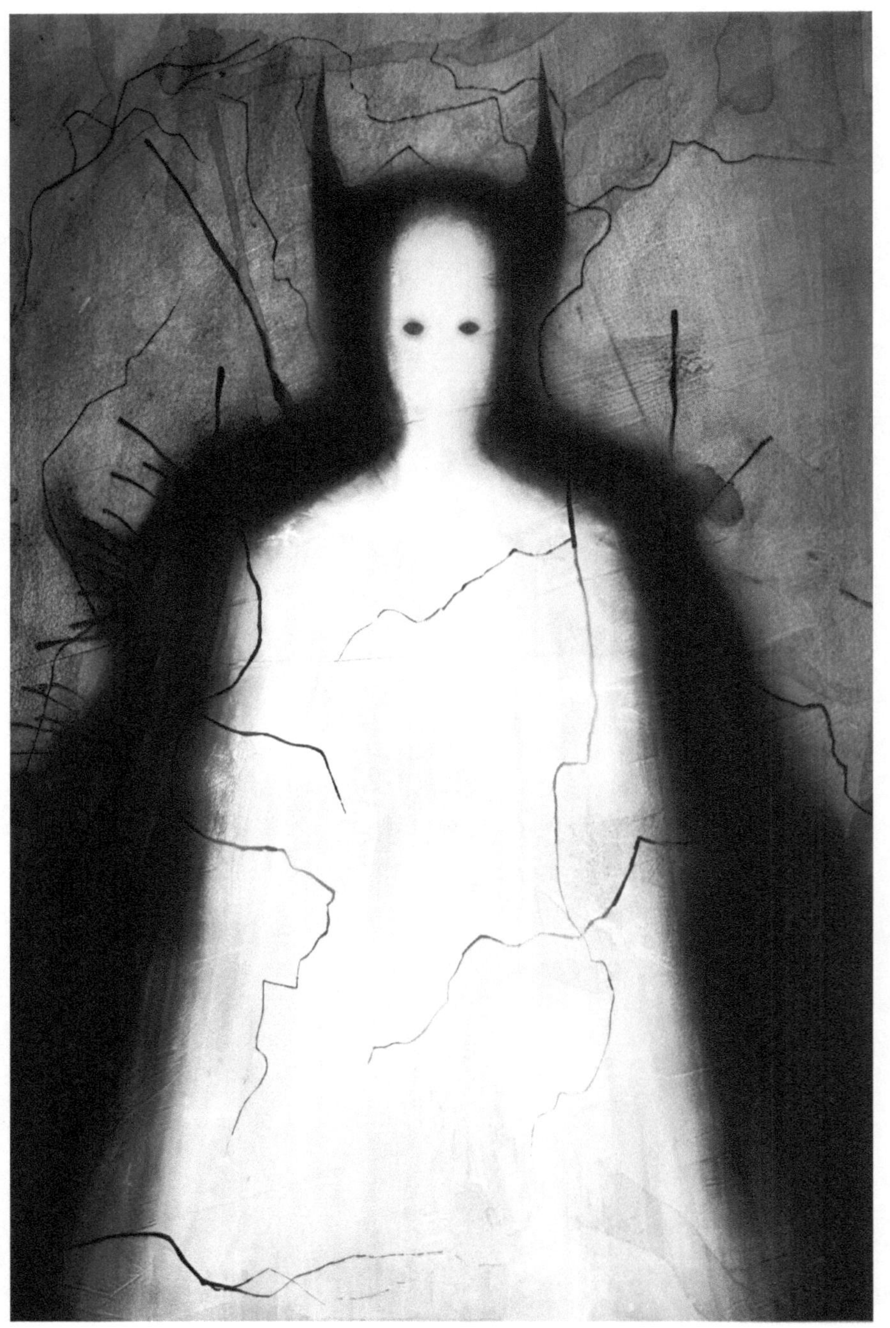

SIGHT

Lenore prepared the baskets to take to the farmer's market. She had cared for her tomatoes all spring and now they were ready to sell. She felt the firmness of each fruit's flesh before they were packaged. She also made small vegetable tarts with thinly-sliced green and yellow squash and her mother's special recipe for pie crust. The day was warming up quickly, so she woke her son, Marcus, to help her load the tomatoes and tarts into the back of his truck. As they drove to the market, Lenore rolled down the window and enjoyed the warmth of the sun on her skin.

Once her table was set up, Marcus kissed his mother's cheek before heading to his job as an electrician. The farmer's market opened up and people slowly trickled into the large community center building where it was held. Lenore fished some cords out of her bag and made bracelets as she waited, knotting the cords into intricate patterns. A few people would come by, and she would smile warmly at them, promising the sweetest vine-ripe tomatoes they ever tasted. She could always tell when someone was genuinely interested in buying something; they always had an orange glow about them.

Lenore had lost her sight when she was only three, but she could still see the colors of folk as they came near. Not the color of their skin, you see, but *their* colors. She could get a feeling for the person she was speaking to, based on the aura they provided her with. She felt she had a better judge of character than those could see and be deceived by outward appearances. Children almost always had a bright white or yellow shine to them, indicative of their youthful energy and curiosity. She enjoyed watching them run about, their sparks dancing in the darkness like little fireflies on a summer night. Once, she met a young boy whose color was a dull greenish-blue. His mother radiated a dark purple and although she spoke sweetly and politely to Lenore, she knew that the woman was sometimes cruel to her boy. Lenore wished there was something she could do, but her gift limited her only to interpretations and insight to the private lives of others.

She was in a transaction with a kindly older couple when she felt something draw her attention elsewhere. Down the line of tables selling baked goods, jams, and eggs, she saw a dark shadow. In the entire spectrum of hues that she saw in people, she had never come across a person like this. It was like a black hole. A bottomless pit sucking the warmth and light from others nearby. She had seen people "share" a glow, usually couples or old friends. This was different. It was as if their glows were being siphoned slowly into darkness, the way spices are absorbed and visually lost in a big pot of simmering sauce. She thanked the couple for the extra dollar in change they told her to keep, and they went on their way.

She watched the dark shadow of a person making its way toward her table. She tried to focus on the bracelet she was working on, but couldn't help but feel a little uneasy. She pulled her shawl closer around her shoulders; it was unusually chilly for August.

"Hello, there." A man's voice. She looked up and saw only darkness before her. "Beautiful tomatoes, I love the way you layered the squash in the pies, too," the voice continued. It was deep but had a gentle quality to it, amplified by a slight accent she couldn't quite identify.

"Thank you, sir," Lenore responded. Her pale eyes swept back and forth, but she couldn't pick out even the tiniest trace of glow. It was unsettling for her. She felt vulnerable, like she had lost her eyesight all over again.

"I hope you don't mind, but may I inquire as to how you lost your vision, ma'am?" the man spoke again, ever so politely. Lenore's fingers went to her cheek, self-consciously. She forgot, sometimes, that her eyes appeared different to other people.

"Oh, sweetie, this is just what the good Lord decided for me." Her hand moved to the gold crucifix around her neck.

"That's certainly a very nice way to think about it," he said, after a pause. Lenore thought she heard laughter in his tone. "Have you ever wished you could change that?"

Lenore had—often. She remembered when she first realized she was different from her family and other children. She was bullied at school for calling the other children by their colors instead of their names. She learnt to keep her gift more private after that. As she grew older, however, she learned to accept and love herself. She also learned to love a man, who gave her a beautiful son and forty-three years of joy before he passed away in their marital bed. "A long time ago," she replied simply.

"I could help you with that, you know. You could see the world in full technicolor vision." Lenore didn't know how to respond to that, unable to tell if he was joking.

"I've seen many doctors throughout my life; ain't none of them ever told me they could give me new eyes. Would you like to purchase some tomatoes or a tart?" The intimacy of the conversation was making her more uncomfortable than she already was, talking to this man with no glow.

"No thank you, ma'am, just browsing." And with that, he left. Lenore felt a sense of weight being lifted off her as he went. She could hear him chatting with Tom, who sold fresh eggs and a variety of mushrooms, at the next table. She and Tom had become well-acquainted over the years, bonding over gardening tips, recipes, and the occasional drought that plagued their crops.

Trying not to eavesdrop, she busied herself by fixing the tangled mess of a bracelet she was working on. A few of Tom's words found their way to Lenore's sensitive ears. "Loan" and "mortgage" carried over the background chatter of the Farmer's Market. She knew Tom had been struggling the past few years. His back just wasn't up for all the maintenance that comes with a farm. His children had moved out years ago and started families of their own in large cities hours away.

Lenore gazed toward the two men and was horrified to see Tom's forest green glow being pulled into the darkness that stood before him. She heard them talking casually as if nothing was wrong. A woman and her children drew her attention back to her table. She sold her two baskets of beautifully fragrant cherry tomatoes and gave her a small paper with a copy of her mother's tomato soup recipe. When she turned back to Tom's table, the darkness was gone. The ambiance of her surroundings had returned to normal.

The following weekend, she noticed that Tom's table was empty. She asked around, but none of the other vendors seemed to know his whereabouts. When Marcus came to collect her, she asked him to stop by at Tom's house. "I want to take him one of my zucchini tarts, in case he's feeling unwell," she said. When they pulled up his drive, she could sense him sitting in his rocking chair on the front porch. She noticed his usual green had turned into a murky blue and knew something was wrong. "How are you, Tom? I missed you today at the market." She spoke softly, holding out the pie dish in her hands. "I thought you might want some food."

"Thank you, Lenore. That's mighty kind of you." His voice sounded strained.

"What's got you down, honey?" Lenore put on her most grandmotherly voice, although Marcus had yet to provide her with a grandbaby of her own. "My oldest son was in a bad car accident," Tom said bluntly.

"Oh, dear!" Lenore exclaimed. "I am so sorry to hear that; is he all right?"

She heard Tom sniffle and knew. "No, uh, he's not." Tom managed to say, his voice tight with pain. "A man... a man stopped by yesterday to deliver the news. Some lawyer who worked in the same firm as my boy. Told me my son had arranged to pay off my farm and equipment a few years back. Put it all in his will." He stopped to collect himself. Lenore's heart ached for the poor man. Tom continued. "That man had a little paper with all the details... and a short note from my son. He wrote it when he made the arrangements."

Lenore reached out and touched Tom's arm. "What did it say?" She could hear rustling as Tom pulled a paper from his breast pocket.

"It said, 'Dad, I love you, but I knew I wouldn't always be able to come home every year to help you with the harvest." Tom struggled to keep his voice steady. "In the event that something happens to me, I've paid off the mortgage on the house and land and left a small amount of rainy-day funds for you to continue living the life you love. I know it won't replace a strong back and an extra pair of hands, but maybe it can replace that old barn you've been meaning to tear down. Love always, Jeremy.'"

Lenore was speechless. It seemed unreal. Then she remembered the man from the market the previous week. "I'm so sorry for your loss, Tom. Really." She gave his arm a squeeze. "I don't mean to change the subject so rudely, but did you recognize that man from last week at the Farmer's Market? I don't think I've ever heard his voice before."

She felt Tom stiffen. "I've never seen him before. He just came up and started asking me about business as a farmer, like he knew I'd been struggling and just wanted to rub it in a little. He was very polite," the old man recollected, "but I couldn't help but feel like he was deliberately asking questions I didn't want to answer."

Lenore knew the exact feeling Tom described. Suddenly, Tom broke down into sobs, crumbling back into his chair. "I killed my son!" he cried. "That man was the Devil, and I knew it when I laid eyes on him. He said he had a way to help with my financial needs and I believed him. He said he'd be in contact with me. I shook his hand. I never would've done it if I knew this was how he meant it." Lenore shushed him and wrapped her arms around him the best she could, but her mind was racing. She asked if there was anything she could do and told him not to hesitate to contact her anytime. Tom thanked her and said he needed to lie down for a while.

As Lenore got back into her son's truck, she was silent. "What's happened, Ma?" Marcus asked as he shifted into reverse and backed out of Tom's driveway.

She reached out and stroked the side of his face. "His son has just passed away, poor soul. We should come back with a decent meal for him tomorrow—I'm thinking a chicken casserole." She spoke absentmindedly, distracted by her own thoughts of that shadowy man. The Devil. "I love you, Marcus," she said, after a long pause. Marcus chuckled.

"I love you too, Ma." He gave her hand a small squeeze.

The next day, the two returned with the casserole. Marcus knocked at the door, but there was no answer. Tom's old Ford pickup was still parked in the driveway, so Marcus took a look around the farm for him while Lenore waited on the porch. Minutes later, Marcus came back to the porch. His glow had turned a sickeningly pale yellow-green. He had found Tom hanging from the rafters in the barn. "He had a sign pinned to his shirt, Ma," Marcus told her, his voice shaking. "God Forgive Me."

BAR SHADOWS

L AST NIGHT, SOMETHING FOLLOWED me home. I left work later than usual. There had been a birthday party and the bar was wrecked by the time I ushered the stragglers out. I sent Beth home around two-thirty because I knew she had a young boy at home. I finished mopping all the sticky surfaces, turned the lights off, and locked up.

The walk home wasn't far, and I was happy to have warm weather coming back. The day had been one of the first nice ones of the year—not quite t-shirt weather yet, but it would be here soon enough. After leaving the bar, I couldn't shake the feeling I was being watched. I glanced around but couldn't see anyone else out on the street. I lived in an older section of the city, so most streets were poorly lit. I've never had any problems walking home this late before. I'm a big guy, and I don't scare easily. Yet that night I found myself looking over my shoulder more than a few times.

Every time I checked behind me, I saw only the empty street I had just walked. Then I heard it—the crunch of broken glass on the pavement. I told myself it must have been a stray cat rustling around in some garbage, but deep down I knew that whatever made that sound had to be much larger than a cat. I quickened my pace, feeling somewhat sheepish for allowing myself to get creeped out. I listened to my footsteps on the sidewalk. The echoes didn't sound quite right. Something *was* following me. I whirled around one more time and finally saw it.

A human figure stood several yards behind me, stark naked. From the distance, it was hard to discern any clear features other than it was a middle-aged male. Under normal circumstances, this wasn't the type of guy that would strike me as a physical threat. In my time as a bouncer, I'd handled men twice his size with ease, drunks and druggies both. But something was off. He was just standing there—staring at me. Goosebumps rippled through my body.

"Are you okay, man?" I called to him. He remained motionless. I gave him a quick wave, just to establish that I was aware of him and continued walking. I could hear him shuffling behind me still. Up ahead, I saw a small gas station-convenience store that was still open. I turned back to him, and he halted once more. "Hey guy, I don't know what your problem is. I don't have any money on me," I said. He was closer than he was the first time I saw him. I turned my back and counted five seconds in my head as I listened to his footsteps before I faced him again.

This time, he was close enough for me to see a few more of his features. His hair was thinning, and his overall physique was gaunt and pale. His skin seemed to hang loosely on his frame... like he had lost weight, but not from exercise. It must've been one helluva drug he was on. Whatever it was, I didn't want to get any closer to him. I jogged ahead to the convenience store, feeling relief wash over me as I stepped into the sterile fluorescent light. I went up to the counter where an acne-ridden guy sat, half asleep. "Jake" was printed on his nametag.

"Hey, can I use your phone? There's a naked junkie outside giving me the creeps," I said to the young man, whose eyes popped open at the word "naked." He peered out through the storefront windows. I could see the man outside, standing across the street just watching me.

"Is this some kind of prank, dude?" Jake started. He stood up to get a better look. "I don't see anything." I looked back and forth between the naked man outside to the greaseball behind the counter.

"Are you kidding me? How can you not see him? He's right there." I pointed at the man outside. Jake shook his head and eyeballed me with suspicion. "He's been following me. I need to use your phone," I continued.

"Look, I'm going to have to ask you to leave if you're not buying anything, sir," Jake said cautiously. "I don't see any naked guy outside, I think you should just go home."

I looked back at the man outside. My apartment was only another few blocks up the street. Jake, the gas attendant, was no help. I pushed my way out the door and took off at a run. At my size, running wasn't something I did often, but I was still certain I could make it home before that crazy person got close enough. I looked over my shoulder as I ran and could see him just walking after me in that same slow, shuffling gait.

I made it to my door and fumbled with the keys. I stood facing the man, or whatever he was, since he never seemed to move when I was looking directly at him. I was correct. He stopped where he was, in the middle of the street. I unlocked the door and slammed it behind me. Looking out the eyehole, I could see the man still standing there in the street. It was like he knew I was still watching him. I double-checked the locks on the door and made my way upstairs to my apartment, finally at ease.

When I went to my window that overlooked the street, I couldn't see the man anymore. Too exhausted to shower, I flopped onto my bed. *What a crazy night,* I thought, as I pulled the sheets up over my shoulders and went to sleep.

I had a disturbing dream that night. I could hear someone in the hallway, slowly making their way up the stairs. With each step they took, I felt cold dread growing inside me. I visualized that naked man climbing the stairs, each footstep heavy. When I went to check the door, it was open a few feet. I closed it and locked it, but when I pulled on the door it opened up easily, despite the fact that I had locked it. I repeated this several times, but in dreams, the laws of physics don't always cooperate. I could hear his ragged breath as he got closer on the stairs. I locked the door one last time and dragged my heavy coffee table over to hold it shut.

The doorknob wiggled. He was outside my door, trying to get in. The lock gave way with ease as it had done during my previous attempts to lock the door. The coffee table stopped the door from opening, but was sliding on the carpet. I leaned my weight against the door, struggling to keep that thing outside.

I woke up in a cold sweat. My apartment was still dark; I had been asleep for only about an hour. The first thing I did was jump out of bed to check my door. It was shut and locked. I breathed a sigh of relief and sat with my back against the door, rubbing the sleep from my eyes. As I was doing so, I heard a small noise inside my apartment. I looked around the room, adrenaline still coursing through my body from the dream. My eyes took a second to adjust after all the rubbing, but when they did, my blood went cold. There, in the far corner, the naked man stood.

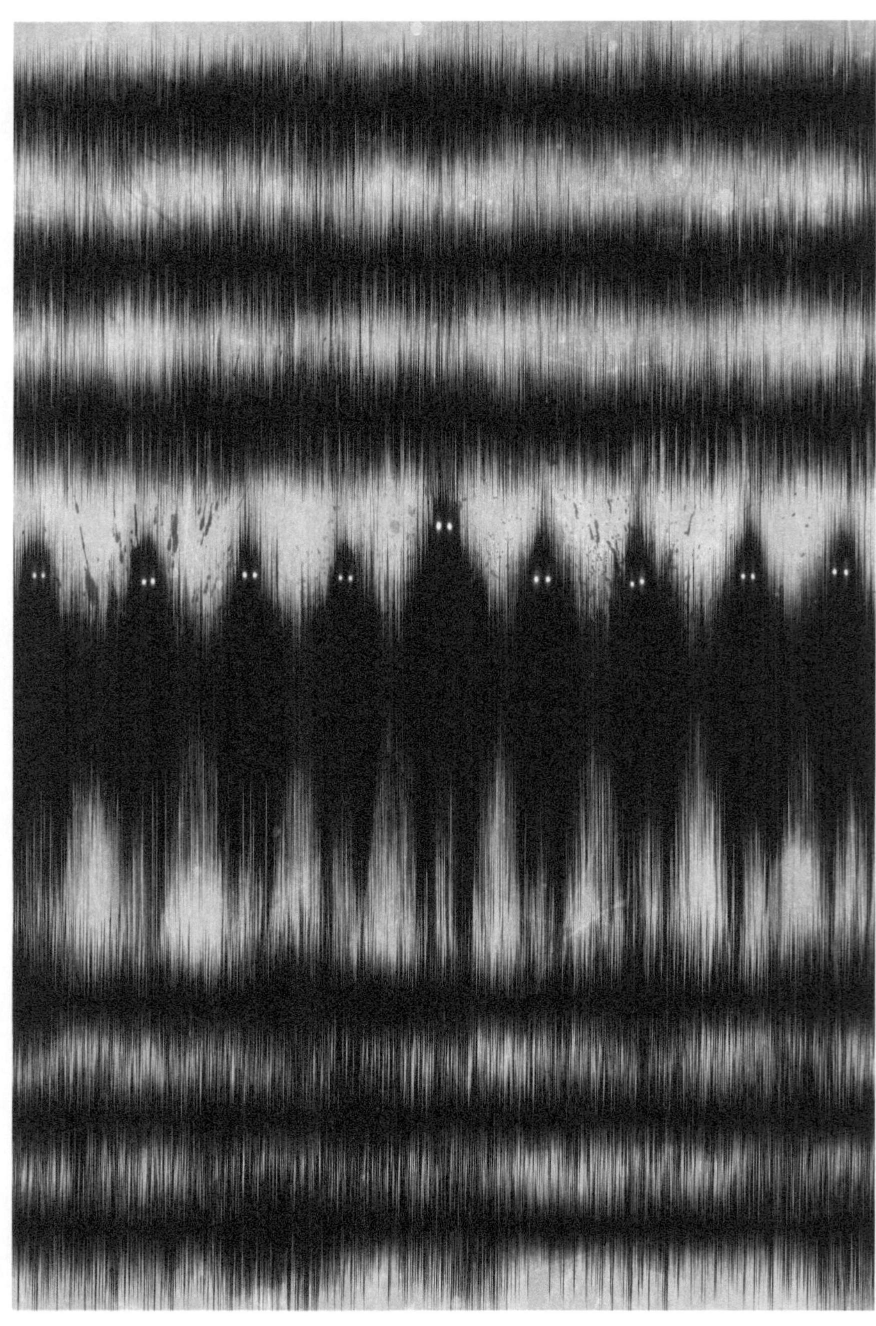

THE CALL

5:47 PM

"Hey honey, it's me. Just wanted to give you a heads-up—I'm running late for dinner. Steve called me in for a last-minute meeting about numbers. I'll be there by 6:15, promise. Love ya. Bye."

6:05 PM

"Me again. Guess you're still on the road. Traffic's insane. I'm ten minutes out, but something's off—fire trucks, cruisers, whole circus. Might be a bad crash. I'll keep you posted. Call me when you get to the restaurant."

6:18 PM

"Julia, pick up. Something's wrong. People are out of their cars, just... wandering in the street. Sirens everywhere. Radio's saying something about a shooting, but nobody knows. I'm boxed in. Call me back. Please."

6:24 PM

"Jesus—listen, don't go outside. Streets aren't safe. My car's stuck at Vancouver and 3rd. I'm heading to the restaurant on foot. If you're there, stay put. People—" [a sudden scuffle, a grunt] *"Hey! Get your fucking hands off—!"* [click]

6:26 PM

"Julia—listen—" His voice ragged, sharp with adrenaline. *"Some asshole came at me—cut my arm. Crazy bastard. Some woman—Jesus, she just cracked his skull open with her stroller. Her fucking stroller. Gunshots everywhere. Where are you? Tell me you're safe."*

6:30 PM

"I found cover," the man was panting as he spoke. *"Dry cleaners on 4th. Place was locked but I busted in through the back. If you can—get here. We'll ride this out together. I hear helicopters. You hear that? It's—"* The sound of rotors thrumming in the background washed out his next words. *"Call me, baby. Please."*

6:31 PM

The man's voice is different now—off.

"Are you ignoring me?" His voice tinged with a sudden snap of anger, wet and raw. *"You're with him, aren't you?"* The man laughed caustically, his next words filled with sharp bitterness. *"You think I don't know? Mike Snyder's penthouse, yeah? The two of you watching the chaos below and laughing? I trusted you, Julia. I loved you—"*

He took a long, heaving breath. Then—something worse. His voice dropped to a guttural tone.

"I'll find you."

His voice was now flat. Hollow. *"I'll find you, you bitch. And I'll cave your skull in—then his."*

6:35 PM

The man's voice was smoothed over now, almost too calm.

"Hey... that was a joke. You know me, babe. Just... stress talking. Everything's fine now. Quiet outside. Call me back, yeah?"

———

Sal shook his head and sighed as he listened to the voicemails again. He had been transcribing audio like this for the past two days. This was the worst instance yet. The other two incidents were much smaller in scale and only lasted a few minutes each. *Whoever is doing this is getting better at it*, he thought. Four months ago, in a small town in Iowa, a grocery store was destroyed when everybody shopping and working there suddenly started to attack each other like animals. Surveillance footage showed the event only lasted 3 minutes but left seven dead, and 13 injured. One month ago, a church outside of Durham, North Carolina, did the same, but this time the ordeal went on for almost 10 minutes. Only 2 survivors, both of whom had been carrying guns. Not a surprise. More than half of the victims in that church died of gunshot wounds.

The Los Angeles incident had lasted roughly a half hour, with at least a third of the city dealing with the carnage and aftermath. It made no sense. The survivors within the affected radius were rounded up and studied by the CDC to look for signs of biological warfare, but their results showed nothing conclusive. Sal's job was to review those areas' archived audio and video footage and search for any common factors that could link the events together.

The voicemail interface glowed on Sal's monitor. His second monitor had the transcription timeline that read: *Los Angeles Out-*

break — April 12, 2028. Sal shook his head. *Christ.* That last voice still crawled under his skin. The other outbreaks had been short, messy... localized. This one—thirty minutes. The official body count was still rising as law enforcement and emergency responders worked relentlessly to find victims and survivors.

Sal clicked his recorder and spoke: "Case Log, Incident Three. Male subject—aggression onset at six minutes. Significant behavioral shift at eight. Hypothesis: audio stimulus triggered hostility. Testing for anomaly."

Sal exhaled and cracked his knuckles. His hands hovered over the keyboard before clicking play again. The voicemail unfolded in its eerie, too-calm way.

"Hey... that was a joke. You know me, babe. Just... stress talking. Everything's fine now. Quiet outside. Call me back, yeah?"

A chill crawled up Sal's spine. No. Not "fine," not "quiet," not with the knowledge of what happened that night. He removed his headphones and rubbed his temples as he pictured the news footage of the carnage that took place in LA.

He was about to slide his headphones on and hit rewind when a soft *tap* against the window made him pause. He turned—*Megan? No—Melissa.* She smiled at him and gave a quick wave before pointing to the vending machine behind her.

New hire, Sal remembered. *Melissa.* He hadn't really *spoken* to her. Didn't know *how.* The office had made it clear she was deaf before she started only two weeks prior and Sal... didn't know ASL. That knowledge, or lack thereof, had rooted him in place, unsure how to break the ice, so he simply... *hadn't.*

She held up her phone to the glass. A message, bold and simple:

"Third time this week! I hate this thing!"

Sal froze. *What do I say?* His chest felt tight, his brain was too loud and too empty all at once. He gave her a quick, stupid, thumbs-up sign and a tight smile before retreating to his seat with his ears burning in quiet embarrassment.

She was *cute.* Probably part of why he felt so *damn awkward.* That, and the quiet guilt gnawing at him—not knowing how to talk to her and worse... *never trying.*

In his soundproof studio, Sal admittedly felt a little isolated from the rest of the office. Before these events began to happen, he worked in an open-air cubicle, processing and transcribing political speeches. He was able to remove his headphones and make small chat with Kenji, the graphics designer who had a dark sense of humor and a huge grin, or Rachel from HR, who sometimes wore too much perfume. They would share light conversations over coffee or lunch breaks. In this room, he could only look through the plate-glass window behind him that opened up to that vending machine in the hallway.

Sal set into his work, isolating background sound profiles from the voice of the man. He heard the chaos in the background, people screaming, glass breaking, gunshots... sirens.

He scrolled back to the previous recording, the first 911 call of that night from the affected area, reporting a car accident.

6:04 PM

"Hello?" The woman's voice was panicked. *"There's been an accident at the intersection of 4th and Vine. Two cars just smashed into each other head-on. I'm going to go check—"*

The audio became jumbled as Sal listened to the woman getting out of her car, frantically asking for help from bystanders. He increased the volume. The words weren't clear, but Sal could pick out the sound of the approaching police sirens in the background.

He skipped to the next recording.

6:12PM

"Hi, this is Paul Drucker, I'm calling from—" The sound of glass shattering cut into the man's words.

"I just witnessed an attack. Paul's voice became more panicky now. *"A man just lunged at a woman walking by. It didn't look like a mugging, he just—"* More background noises cut his words off.

"...looked like he bit her face. She—oh, my god. She's digging her thumbs into his eyes. Please, send help right now!"

As Sal listened to it, he could hear the approaching sirens of the first responders as they arrived.

The sirens, he thought. His mind whirred as his fingers frantically stabbed at his keyboard. It was a stretch, but he needed to isolate the sound of the sirens. Something came through when he heard them in the background from these three calls. He needed to listen to it again.

He switched to the spectrogram view on his second monitor, the colors shifting as the frequency spectrum unraveled in slow motion before his eyes. The sirens were there, bright bands of energy cutting across the timeline like open wounds.

But something else was there, too.

Sal narrowed the frequency range, applying a band-pass filter to isolate just the sirens. Normally, this would remove the human voices, allowing him to focus on background noise. He adjusted the Q factor, tightened the filter, and replayed the audio.

The sirens rang out, clean and crisp, but underneath them... a pulse. Sal's gut twisted. *That shouldn't be there.*

He leaned in, his forearms resting against his cold stainless-steel desk, pulling up the waveform display on his second monitor. The sirens formed predictable oscillations—but this new frequency was irregular. *Layered.* He boosted the gain on the anomaly.

A whisper of distortion bled through his headphones. No, not a whisper. *A voice.*

Sal ripped his headphones off, taking a moment as thoughts spiraled throughout his head. His heart pounded in his chest.

It was probably just an artifact, he reassured himself. Some kind of digital ghost from compression. That happened all the time. That had to be it. He swallowed hard, his throat going dry.

You need to drink more water, he scolded himself. It can get lonely in an isolated office, so Sal had to entertain his mind by talking to himself at times.

He thought about making a trip out to the vending machine to grab a beverage, but something kept him at his desk. He put his headphones back on and clicked the spectral subtraction button, trying to strip away the sirens completely. The background noise collapsed, but the whisper remained.

His breath came faster now. This wasn't compression noise. This wasn't static. It was a voice, and it was saying something... almost *singing*. Sal's fingers hovered over the keyboard. His pulse pounded in his ears as the whisper from the Los Angeles tape echoed in his mind. He felt it in his bones—this wasn't random. With a few quick commands, he pulled up the archived files of the Iowa grocery store incident from December, and the Church in Durham from March.

His throat felt tight as he opened the Iowa file first. The audio hissed to life.

A woman's frantic voice: *"...shelves just fell, people are fighting—my god, he's biting him—"*

Sal's jaw clenched. He skipped forward, isolating the background. He applied the same high-pass filter, clearing the chaos and honing in on the upper frequencies and there it was, the sirens. Underneath, though... a familiar, unnatural pulse, buried deep beneath the wail.

Sal's stomach knotted. His fingers moved faster, pulling up the Durham recording.

A man's panicked voice: "They're shooting inside the church! Please, Lord, save us from this—"

Sal stripped the voice from the mix, running a spectral analysis once more. The sirens... *and that same pulse.*

His hands trembled as he overlaid all three spectrograms: Iowa. Durham. Los Angeles. The sirens—identical. Same harmonic distortion. Same hidden frequency. Same inhuman resonance—like the sirens were screaming back. The spectrogram lines from LA, Durham, and Iowa aligned perfectly. Same spikes and the same unnatural modulation. It was a pattern, not an anomaly. This was no coincidence. Sal's breath hitched, and he felt a sharp sting in his nose. He wiped at it and froze. His fingertips came away wet and dark. *Blood.*

A sudden, high-pitched whine bloomed in his ears—like the sirens were inside his head. His vision blurred. His chest heaved. He scrambled to pause the audio, but his fingers fumbled.

The pulse—he could feel it. Throbbing, vibrating in his skull.

"Shut up. *Shut up!*" he hissed, his voice shaking.

The whisper from the LA recording seemed to rise from the speakers, distorting, bending—until it almost sounded like his own name. *Sal...* it called to him. He hit the keyboard with his fist, finally stopping the audio. The whine stopped and Sal's office plunged into silence except for his shallow, rattling breaths. For a moment, he almost thought he was about to rip his entire setup off of his desk and throw it against the wall.

He grabbed a few tissues from the box on his desk and held them against his nose, tilting his head back in his chair, feeling lightheaded. Despite being able to review video footage of people savagely attacking one another, he had no tolerance for seeing blood in "real life."

At that moment, a muffled crash from behind made Sal whirl around, yanking his headphones off in the process. Kenji was punching the vending machine. No—*slamming his fists into it*, his knuckles splitting open on the glass. Blood streaked down the machine's surface, mixing with shattered plastic from the busted keypad. Sal stood up and ran to the window, confused, when Joe from accounting rushed into the hallway. He grabbed Kenji around the waist, wrestling him away from the machine.

Then Kenji turned his head and bit into Joe's jaw.

Sal saw the skin stretch, then split, as teeth punctured flesh like overripe fruit. An arterial spray painted the wall and side of the vending machine in wide, uneven streaks.

Sal stumbled a few steps back from the window now, hands clamped over his mouth. His mind refused to process what he was seeing.

Joe jerked away, or tried to—but Kenji's teeth stayed latched, pulling a long strip of tissue with him. Joe collapsed onto his side, mouth moving, his voice just a muffled gargle through the glass. His hands pressed weakly against his neck, blood welling between his fingers like syrup.

A sudden blur of movement—Janet, the head of marketing, sprinted into the hallway. Sal barely registered the moment before she tackled Rachel from HR to the floor, claws digging into her scalp. Rachel screamed, or at least her mouth did, but through the thick glass, there was only silence. Then Janet started slamming Rachel's head against the tile.

Again.

And again.

And again.

On the third impact, Rachel's skull cracked open, her legs kicking out, grasping for traction on the tile floor. Blood seeped outward, pooling into the grout lines.

Kenji, his mouth dripping red, turned his head sharply—as if sensing movement. Then he lunged at Janet, sending both of them crashing into the vending machine. The already cracked glass shattered inward, shards embedding in their skin, but neither seemed to notice.

More figures poured into the hallway, frenzied and animalistic. Sal backed away from the window even further, chest heaving. He couldn't hear any of it. Not the screams, not the bones snapping, not the wet, pulpy impacts—only the sound of his own ragged breathing.

Then Melissa came into view, and Sal knew—she was already dead.

She sprinted into the blood-soaked hallway, her shoes skidding in the growing pools of crimson. She froze, her face contorting from confusion to raw terror as her eyes met the carnage—Kenji tearing at Janet's neck, Joe twitching in a heap, the floor slick with the aftermath of primal violence.

Sal slammed his hands against the glass. "RUN!" he screamed, his voice swallowed by the soundproof barrier.

Melissa's eyes snapped to his as if she could hear him—wide, desperate, like a deer's eyes. Quickly, her fingers blurred across her phone. She pressed it hard against the glass—"Help me" flashing on her screen. She pounded her fists against the barrier, her mouth shaped the words Sal couldn't hear in silent pleas. But he didn't move. He couldn't. Her eyes flicked to his office door, then back to him.

"Open it," her lips begged. "Open it!" The door wouldn't open unless a key card with access was swiped first.

The others, *those who still stood*, turned toward her. Bloodied, broken bodies moved with slow, eerie unity, their eyes glassy, their faces masks of feral hunger. The nearest, Kenji, face red with gore, twitched, then charged.

Melissa's eyes widened and in that instant... Sal locked the deadbolt.

Her face crumpled, the plea twisting into betrayal. She knew what he had done. Her lips formed his name, one final, soundless scream—"*Sal!*"

Then the swarm hit her. Arms dragged her down in a blur of clawing hands and snapping jaws. She fought hard—fists flailing, nails clawing, teeth bared—but the weight crushed her, and she vanished beneath them.

Sal stood, trembling, his breath fogging the blood-streaked glass. Then the hallway went still. Everyone still alive stood up as if they had just woken from a deep sleep, shocked at the horrors surrounding them.

Sal watched their faces, some of them retched, spilling their lunch onto the bloodied floor. From his office, Sal could only hear his heartbeat, deafening in his ears. On the glass, he could see Melissa's handprint, smeared in the blood as her final touch.

ABOUT THE AUTHOR

Dᴀɴᴀ Nᴏʀᴀᴀs ᴡʀɪᴛᴇs ʜᴏʀʀᴏʀ, mostly because it gives her an excuse to stare into the void and call it "research." She was raised on *Goosebumps*, *Scary Stories to Tell in the Dark*, and the creeping suspicion that something was watching her from the hallway. Then came Stephen King, and things got worse—in the best way.

She works as an entertainment journalist covering film and television, with a soft spot for anything that might reasonably be described as "unsettling." Her first short story collection, *Lingering Things and Other Dark Tales*, was originally published in 2018.

She lives in Northeastern Pennsylvania with her partner, a collection of horror movies, and the overwhelming sense that she's forgetting something important.

ABOUT THE ILLUSTRATOR

DAVE DICK IS AN illustrator specializing in eerie and dark artwork. He is based in Philadelphia and creates creepy images that are found somewhere between nightmare and reality. When he is not bringing shadows to the page, he is watching movies, wrangling his two kids, or spending time with his wife, who puts up with his dark obsession and esoteric quirks.

Visit Dave online: DaveDickIllustration.com

MORE CHILLS FROM VELOX BOOKS

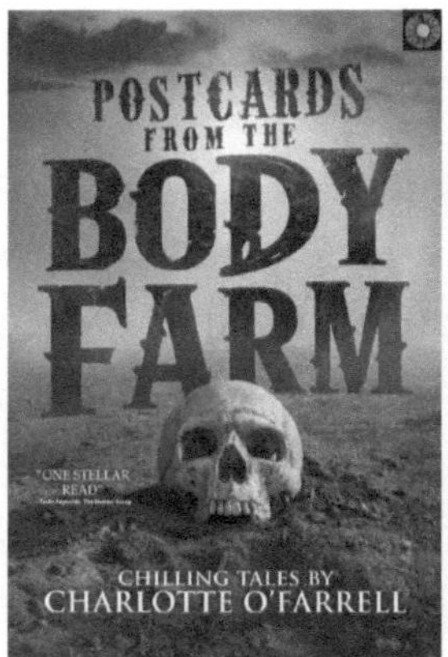

MORE CHILLS FROM VELOX BOOKS

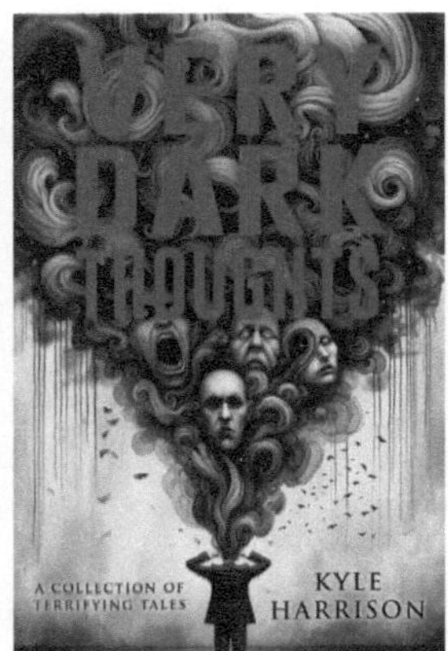